Seduced by the Monster

Seduced by the Monster

Highland Shifters Book 4

Caroline S. Hilliard

Copyright © 2022 by Cathrine T. Sletta (aka Caroline S. Hilliard)

All rights reserved.

This publication is the sole property of the author, and may not be reproduced, as a whole or in portions, without the express written permission of the author. This publication may not be stored in a retrieval system or uploaded for distribution to others. Thank you for respecting the amount of work that has gone into creating this book.

Produced in Norway.

This book is a work of fiction and the product of the author's imagination. Names, characters, organizations, locations, and events are either the product of the author's imagination or used fictitiously. Any resemblance to actual persons, living or dead, organizations, events or locations is purely coincidental.

ISBN: 979-8-8368-1628-5

Copy edited by Lia Fairchild

Cover design by Munch + Nano
Thank you for creating such a beautiful cover for my story.

CONTENTS

About this book	i
Chapter 1	1
Chapter 2	13
Chapter 3	24
Chapter 4	33
Chapter 5	43
Chapter 6	57
Chapter 7	65
Chapter 8	72
Chapter 9	87
Chapter 10	100
Chapter 11	113
Chapter 12	121
Chapter 13	130
Chapter 14	140
Chapter 15	154
Chapter 16	160

Chapter 17	172
Chapter 18	179
Chapter 19	194
Chapter 20	210
Chapter 21	217
Chapter 22	231
Chapter 23	242
Epilogue	254
Books by Caroline S. Hilliard	262
About the author	263

ABOUT THIS BOOK

His true mate has arrived on his doorstep. But will she accept him, knowing that losing control of her emotions can be fatal?

Sabrina has never met a man who has enticed her the way Leith does. He threatens her carefully honed control. Strong emotions are something of the past, and she can never allow herself to truly feel again. Ever. It's a fact she has accepted and learned to live with. And she can't change that, not even for the man of her dreams. Not when the consequences can prove fatal.

Leith knows immediately who she is. His true mate. The moment he has been anticipating for most of his long life has finally arrived. But what he expected to be the first day of their happily ever after, turns out to be a test even with his considerable patience. He can see that she wants him as much as he wants her, but her need for control may be greater than her need for true love.

This work is intended for mature audiences. It contains explicit sexual situations and violence that some readers may find disturbing.

CHAPTER 1

Sabrina stood in water that reached to just above her nipples and stared out across Loch Ness. It was midnight, and the sliver of a moon gave her just enough light to see the smooth surface of the water stretched out before her. The ripples from what she had seen breaking the surface a couple of minutes ago were gone, and all that was left was the image in her mind of what she had witnessed. The smooth curve of a large body rising silently from the water before disappearing again.

Another couple of minutes went by as she stood there hoping whatever it was would surface once more. Perhaps this time showing more than just its back, or what she assumed had been the creature's back. She had no idea what it was she had seen, but the story of the Loch Ness monster came to mind. It couldn't be, though. It was just a story to lure the tourists.

For some reason she wasn't scared at all. Standing

naked in the black water all alone, she felt perfectly safe. And why wouldn't she be? Humans weren't on the menu for anything that lived in the loch, no matter how big the fish might get.

Sighing with disappointment, Sabrina turned and walked back to the beach where her clothes and towel were lying. The large creature or fish had obviously moved on. She grabbed the towel and quickly dried off before wrapping it around her to cover her nakedness. Then, she picked up her clothes and started walking back to Leith's house.

Thankfully, nobody had locked the downstairs entrance to the house while she was gone. She walked silently down the hallway before entering her bedroom. It was a small, beautifully decorated room at the bottom level of the house, right next to the master bedroom. All the other bedrooms in the house were occupied by couples, so it made sense that she was given the smallest room. According to Leith, the small room was going to be a nursery one day, when the man of the house found his mate.

Sabrina got into bed and closed her eyes, but it didn't take long for them to pop back open. Staring up at the ceiling in the dark room, she lay on her back as thoughts churned in her mind, preventing sleep from claiming her. So much had happened in the last few days, and the reality of it all was only now starting to sink in.

Shifters. There were shifters in this world. People who could change into animals and who possessed a lot of power. Power similar to, but not the same as, her witch powers. It shouldn't have come as a surprise to her. Sabrina had always known there were people out there with different power signatures from her own, but she had always assumed they were witches or warlocks of some kind not yet known to her. But like she had been taught early on, assumption was the mother of all fuck-ups, and once again it proved to be correct.

Shifters weren't the only type of supernatural beings in addition to witches that existed, apparently, but she didn't know much about the other types yet. Hopefully, she would be able to find out more. It was all very intriguing and perhaps a little scary.

Not nearly as scary as the attractive man sleeping in the bedroom next to hers, though. Or that wasn't correct. Leith wasn't scary at all. That was the problem. He was the most amazing man she had ever met. What was scary was the effect he had on her.

Sabrina knew very well that she had to stay away from him. He wasn't for her. Never could be. But just the few hours they had spent together so far, told her that staying away was going to be extremely difficult. And the way he looked at her and acted around her didn't make it any easier.

If she had a choice, Sabrina would leave first thing in the morning and never return. It would be the best option, the safest option. And if it wasn't for the fact that she was on vacation with Julianne, her best friend, Sabrina would do just that. But leaving her best friend wasn't really an option. Even considering her friend was mated to a handsome and powerful wolf shifter who knew how to take care of her. Sabrina had full confidence in Duncan's ability to care for Julianne and keep her safe, but the events of the last few days were enough to prevent Sabrina from leaving.

Sighing heavily, she turned over on her side. The bed was soft and comfortable, and if Sabrina hadn't been so antsy, she would have slept like a baby. But she couldn't convince her mind to settle. It had been stuck in overdrive ever since they arrived at Leith's house earlier in the day, and she had met the man of the house. The memories of meeting him for the first time replayed in her head.

Duncan, Julianne, and Sabrina had reached Leith's house around midday. His three-level terraced house was beautifully situated by the southeastern shore of Loch Ness. After getting out of the car, Sabrina had been standing with her back to the house and hadn't noticed the owner coming out to welcome them. Leith's voice as he greeted Duncan had flowed over her like a warm caress, immediately making her feel welcome and wanted. It was a strange feeling that had her turning around to get a look at the man with the remarkable voice.

Leith's appearance had been no less remarkable than his voice. He was tall and lean, yet his bare arms revealed corded muscle. Sabrina had a feeling his muscular arms were indicative of the condition of the rest of his body, and just the thought had her blushing like a teenager. Then his dark-green gaze captured hers, and it was like time stopped as she drowned in the pool of his warm gaze. His soft lips brushing over her knuckles in an antiquated yet charming greeting added to the blissful feeling. And if Leith had pulled her into his arms right there and kissed her, a minute after they had met for the first time, she would have let him.

Sabrina pulled in a shaky breath and rolled onto her

back as she pushed the image of his dark-green eyes away. These thoughts weren't helping her sleep. On the contrary, the memories had her heart racing with all the emotions swirling through her body. She had never desired a man before, at least not like this. And it was making her both scared and excited. Not a good combination of feelings for her. She needed to stay in control. It was paramount and something she had perfected for many years. How could one man shake her foundations so thoroughly within just seconds of meeting him?

∞∞∞

Leith was trying to rest, but it was proving difficult. And there was a good reason. An excellent reason. With a beautiful model-perfect face, long blond hair, and big blue eyes. The way her eyes had widened as she first laid eyes on him had made his heart sing with joy because he knew exactly whom she was. He would have known her no matter where they had met, since she had been in his dreams for several decades already. Not her image, but her power signature.

Sabrina was his mate. She didn't know it yet, but she would. In time, when she became receptive to the idea. For now, he would care for her while keeping his distance. Or as much distance as he was able to. It was proving much more difficult than he had thought to stay away from her. His body was already telling him to claim her, even though they had just met.

Sitting up in bed, he sighed in frustration. If only he could get some sleep, but he could tell it wasn't going to happen. The sky was already starting to lighten with the impending dawn, and even though the nights were short in Scotland during summer, and he should try to get a couple of hours sleep before facing the new day, Leith knew he would only be tossing and turning if he tried.

After swinging his legs over the side of the bed, he got to his feet and slowly walked to the bathroom door. The house was completely silent even with all the newly mated couples staying with him. Apparently, newly mated couples needed sleep at times too. Not that he would have heard a lot of noise if they were awake. The soundproofing in his house was significantly better than in the average Scottish dwelling. He had made sure of that when he built the place many years ago.

After finishing in the bathroom, Leith walked back into his bedroom and grabbed a fresh T-shirt and shorts. It was too early for coffee, but he still wanted some. Needed some even. He would make himself a cup and bring it down to the beach to greet the morning sun and enjoy the silence before everyone started moving around. He appreciated his friends visiting, old as well as new, but he was also a person who enjoyed time by himself, and he was going to use this opportunity to revel in the temporary silence.

Exiting his bedroom, he stopped and stared at the door to Sabrina's room. He wouldn't mind her company at the beach, but she needed her sleep. Waking her at this hour was no less than cruel. In time they would be together, and hopefully it wouldn't be too long before that happened. But he sensed both her attraction to him and her resistance to the feeling. There was something holding her back from embracing her budding feelings for him.

Then again, they had met for the first time less than twenty-four hours ago. It was a bit soon to expect her to understand what was going on between them. Leith knew she was his mate, but she had no idea what she was to him. If she had been a shifter, she would have known, but she wasn't. Sabrina was a witch and a powerful one at that.

Leith made his way to the kitchen and started the coffee machine. The kitchen was located at the top level of the house, and he was happy he had made the choice to give the room the prime location in the house. The view of Loch Ness and the western side of the loch was magnificent, and it was even better from the terrace outside the kitchen.

The basis for his choice was that he wanted the kitchen to be the main room for entertaining guests. And in time it would also be a family room, where his mate and their children would spend most of their time when they were home. That was why the kitchen was a large room with all modern appliances and a large kitchen island, a long dining table comfortably seating ten people, a large old-fashioned hearth, and a couple of comfortable sofas and a low table by the windows.

Holding his large steaming mug of coffee in one hand, he turned off the lights as he exited the kitchen. The sun had yet to climb over the horizon, and he wanted to be at the beach before it did. He descended the stairs silently to the lowest level of the house, then came to an abrupt halt when he saw Sabrina stepping out of her room.

"Oh." She started as she saw him before chuckling

softly. "You startled me. I didn't expect to see anyone up this early. Do you usually get up before the sun?"

Leith took in her immaculate appearance before giving her a single shake of his head. "No, not usually. I had trouble sleeping, so I decided to greet the sun on the beach before everyone else started moving about. Would you like to join me?"

Sabrina's eyes widened, and a look of panic was visible on her face for a second, before she schooled her features into a neutral expression. "I… Are you sure you'd like the company?"

Leith kept his eyes on her while giving her a single nod. "Yes, I am sure. I would be honored if you chose to accompany me to the beach." He lifted his hand holding the large mug of coffee. "I made coffee." Leith was perfectly aware that he was putting some pressure on her to join him, but if that was what it took to get to spend some time with her alone, he wasn't going to feel bad about it.

"Um, okay." Sabrina's eyes dropped to the coffee mug as she answered.

"Good." Leith walked over to the external door and opened it. He held it open to let Sabrina exit ahead of him. As she moved past him, he pulled in a breath, and her scent almost made him groan with bliss. Green apples and cinnamon. It was his new favorite scent.

After following her out of the house, he got into step beside her as she walked down the path toward the beach.

"How long have you been living here?" Sabrina didn't look at him when she asked the question.

He debated what to tell her but decided to tell her

the truth. She already knew about shifters and their extended lifespans. "A long time. The house is older than it looks. I have modernized it four times since I built it more than one hundred years ago."

Her head snapped around, and she stared at him. No sound came out when she opened her mouth as if to say something. Then she closed it and turned her head back to stare in the direction she was going.

Leith knew she had wanted to ask him a question, but before uttering the words, she had stopped herself. Perhaps because she thought it would be impolite to ask. "I am old, Sabrina. Much older than Trevor and Duncan. They are no more than toddlers compared to me."

"Okay." Sabrina's facial expression was back to its default neutral. "Can I ask what you mean by old, or would you like not to answer that?"

"I will be happy to answer just about any question you may have, Sabrina. All you need to do is ask. I was born in 1711, a few kilometers north of here." Leith studied her face as he spoke, but there was no visible reaction to his revelation. But he had already stressed the fact that he was old, so perhaps the element of surprise was gone. "I have lived a long time and experienced many things. Hopefully, it has made me wiser instead of indifferent."

The corner of Sabrina's mouth curved a little with her smile. "I'm sure it has. Indifferent is not a word I would use to describe you."

They reached the beach, and Leith pointed at the rocks he usually used to sit on when he came down to the water to relax. "Take a seat, my angel."

Nodding, Sabrina didn't meet his eyes. She chose a

rock and sat down before staring out over the loch.

Leith sat down on a smaller rock next to the one she had chosen, which had him at her eye level. "Would you like some coffee? I only made the one cup since I wasn't aware that you were awake, but I want you to have it. Or we can share." It might be too intimate for her to share a cup, but he decided to try his luck anyway.

"Thank you, Leith." She met his eyes for a second before moving her gaze to the cup. "You do love your coffee, don't you."

It was more of a statement than a question, but as she took the cup from him and lifted it to her mouth, her eyes rose to his like she was waiting for an answer.

Holding her gaze, he nodded once. "I have loved coffee since I first tasted it as a boy. Coffee, beer, and whiskey are my drinks of choice."

Sabrina handed him the cup and smiled. "I like whiskey. I don't drink much alcohol, but I sometimes enjoy a small glass of whiskey when I'm alone." Her smile died on her lips, and her eyes widened as she uttered the last word, like she had just realized what she was saying.

"Only when you are alone?" Judging by her expression, Leith knew he was asking her a question she probably didn't want to answer, but if he was going to get to know his future mate, he had to push her a little. Sabrina wasn't the type of person to volunteer a lot of information about herself and her preferences. And the less he knew about her, the easier it would be for her to slip away from him.

He had never even considered the possibility that his mate would be skittish and reluctant to accept him.

It was a scenario he hadn't been prepared for when meeting Sabrina.

Her gaze dropped to her feet, and a frown marred her delicate brows. "I… I can't let my guard down around people. I need to stay in control."

"Your level of control is admirable, my angel." Leith kept his eyes on her face, but she didn't raise her gaze to his. "I do not think I have met anyone less likely to slip up and make a mistake in judgement. It might seem premature to make that statement after knowing you for less than a day, but I am confident that I am right in my assessment."

"If only." Sabrina's eyes shot to his, and the pain in them floored him. "It only takes one second to hurt someone and change their life forever, Leith. One second."

She was on her feet and walking away from him before he had time to process her words and her pain.

"Sabrina." He shot up from his seat, and the cup dropped from his hand as he sped to catch up with her. "My angel, wait."

She stopped but didn't turn to him.

"I am sorry, Sabrina, if my words made you recall bad memories. Just remember that we all slip up at some time or other. None of us are perfect, and quite a few of us are lethal if we lose control. Even humans with no special abilities can be lethal if they lose control at the wrong moment." Leith wanted to pull her into his arms to comfort her, but he sensed she wouldn't let him if he tried. It would be a comfort to him to hold her close, but this wasn't about him. He wasn't the one who needed to feel safe to open up.

"Thank you for your kind words, Leith." Her head

turned, and blue eyes met his. "It's nice to know that I'm not alone, but it doesn't change the fact that I hurt someone, and that person will forever be altered because of my actions. The fact that I didn't mean it didn't change the outcome."

He gave her a short nod. "I understand, and please know that you can talk to me about anything. I would like nothing better than to be able to help you. But it is your choice, my angel."

She opened her mouth. But before uttering a word, she closed it again and averted her eyes. It seemed like she had been about to tell him something but then decided against it. Whether it was out of old habit or because she didn't trust him yet, he didn't know.

The sun chose that moment to clear the mountains and shine its first rays on the mountaintops across the loch. It drew Sabrina's gaze, and he let his eyes linger on her face, while she was otherwise engaged, taking in the small smile that grew and slowly replaced the sadness from her expression. The way her lips curved with her smile pulled his gaze to them, and he felt an almost uncontrollable urge to taste them. Just a small taste to satisfy his hunger for his mate. But she wasn't ready for that. Not yet.

"So beautiful." Sabrina suddenly turned her head toward him and sought his gaze, but not sure what she would find there, he quickly looked away.

"It is." His voice came out deeper than usual. "I have lived here for more than three hundred years, but I never get tired of the view."

CHAPTER 2

Sabrina was stunned at the level of heat clearly visible in Leith's eyes before he quickly looked away from her. His eyes were shining like emeralds, something she was quickly learning indicated one of two things. Either he was using his power, or he was turned on. And at the moment the latter was true.

She already knew he liked her, even wanted her. But it still rattled her to see the proof of his desire. She was trying to tell herself she didn't like it and didn't want to see the evidence of it in her eyes or…other places on his body. But it was a lie. The heat in his eyes sent a thrill through her, causing her to want things she had never allowed herself to want before. Or at least not since she was sixteen and didn't know what her powers could do.

Ever since *the incident* she had been steering clear of any man who made her look twice. She had dated and even had relationships, but it had all been done to try to feel normal and not because she'd had any real romantic interest in any of the men. Because romantic interest, or lust for that matter, wasn't something she could allow herself to feel. Any emotions that could disrupt her control were forbidden. It was a self-imposed restriction she had never broken. And she had never really been tempted. Until Leith.

She wanted to kiss him. Press herself against his body, pull his head down to her and lick his lips slowly before diving into the kiss with everything she was. His body would feel solid against hers. His lean, strong body wouldn't give an inch as she leaned against him and let her hands roam his washboard abs and hard chest.

Sabrina mentally shook herself to snap out of her thoughts. Being around this man was getting more difficult by the second, it seemed. She had to get a grip and stop spending time alone with him. The best option would be to leave and go back to London, but the thought of not seeing him again made goosebumps break out all over her body, almost like she was cold or scared even though she was neither.

"You're cold." Leith's gaze was on her forearms where she had rolled up her shirtsleeves. "We should go back to the house and make some more coffee." His gaze rose to hers, and his dark-green eyes were filled with concern for her.

Nodding, she smiled at him. But she could feel that it didn't reach her eyes. It would have been amazing to be able to give in and accept Leith's non-verbal invitation to be with him, and the fact that she couldn't was starting to upset her to such an extent it alone might cause her to lose control.

She started when he grabbed her hand and pulled

her toward the house like a man with a mission. But instead of yanking her hand from his grip, she found herself walking beside him like it was the most natural thing in the world. It wasn't, though—far from it.

Sabrina couldn't remember ever walking hand in hand with a man before. That wasn't the kind of relationships she'd been in. They had been amicable, and one of the men she had been with had harbored some romantic feelings for her despite her efforts to prevent that from happening. But mostly she had been arm-candy. For some it might seem degrading for a woman to be treated more like a trophy than a girlfriend, but she had preferred it. No real attachment but still a chance to be with someone and an excuse to go places where couples went.

Too much inside her own head and not watching where she was going, she stepped on a rock, and it rolled out from under her foot. Her ankle twisted, and her leg gave as pain shot through her ankle. Moaning, she braced herself as her body tilted sideways.

She never hit the ground. Strong arms caught her and brought her against a body that was just as hard as she had imagined. And standing on one foot, she couldn't help leaning against him and using his strong hold on her to keep her balance.

"Are you all right?" Leith's concerned gaze met hers when she tipped her head back to look up at him.

"Yes." She nodded absently, the experience of being in his arms stealing her sanity and robbing her vocabulary. Explaining about her ankle would have been the natural thing to do, but the words eluded her as she drowned in his eyes.

"My angel." His voice was deeper than before, and

his eyes quickly brightened into emerald.

The heat in his eyes was mesmerizing, but Sabrina still found her gaze dipping to his lips. They were slightly parted and looked so soft.

A shiver ran through her as his lips moved closer to hers, but it was taking too long. She gripped his shirt and rose up on her toes, putting her other foot down to help her close the distance between them.

Less than an inch separated their lips, when pain shot through her ankle. A small cry left her as she quickly shifted her weight back onto her uninjured leg and tipped her head forward to rest her forehead against his shoulder.

"Sabrina?" His arms tightened around her, and he leaned his cheek against her head. "Did you hurt your leg when you tripped?"

"Yes." She moaned the word into his shirt as pain hammered in her ankle. Then, her world suddenly tilted when Leith lifted her into his arms.

He carried her toward the house, holding her close with one arm hooked behind her back and the other under her knees. "We should put some ice on your leg to reduce the swelling, or the pain will only get worse."

Staring up at him, she nodded. But his focus was on where he was going and not on her. "Yes, ice would be good."

He gave a short nod as was his normal response. "Can you open the door for us?"

Sabrina grabbed the door handle and opened the door, and Leith carried her into the house before ascending the stairs. He carried her like she weighed no more than a feather, and even though she knew he had a shifter's strength, she was still surprised when they reached the top floor of the house, and his breathing was still slow and even.

"What kind of shifter are you?" The question dropped out of her mouth, and she stiffened as she realized what she had just done. Contrary to her own intentions, she had already asked him how old he was, giving him an opening to ask her a personal question in return. By asking another one, she had inadvertently given him permission to ask her whatever he wanted to know about her, and she couldn't reasonably refuse to answer without being disrespectful.

The corner of his mouth curved a little in what constituted a smile for him, as he carried her into the kitchen. "I will show you in time, my angel. For now I think it best if we just focus on getting to know each other."

She should be relieved at his words, as it freed her from the responsibility to answer every question he might choose to ask. But she wasn't. Instead, she felt oddly disappointed and hurt that he didn't trust her with his secret.

Perhaps she had misunderstood his interest, and this was his way of telling her she was getting too close. She was usually very good at perceiving other people's intentions and even thoughts to a certain degree, but Leith wasn't an ordinary man. Maybe she had projected her own attraction onto him, just assuming he was feeling as strongly about her as she was feeling about him. It wasn't impossible. She had misjudged people before. It just didn't happen very often.

Leith carefully lowered her onto the couch by the windows before meeting her gaze. The frown that formed on his face told her she hadn't hidden what she was feeling fast enough to escape his detection.

"Please do not be hurt, my angel." His eyes were begging her to understand as he went down on one knee on the floor beside her. "It is a secret I rarely share, and then only with people I have known for a long time. You will know everything about me in time, but with the knowledge comes great responsibility, and I do not want to burden you with that so soon in our courtship."

Sabrina's heart skipped a beat at his last word, and she wasn't able to hide her shock as both joy and denial surged through her. "But we're not... We'll never..." Unable to find the appropriate words, she stopped.

Leith's eyes suddenly darkened, and his expression changed into one she hadn't seen on his face before. Determination and something like possessiveness hardened his features, and she sucked in a breath as heat unexpectedly raced through her.

"We are courting, Sabrina. Make no mistake about that." Leith had captured her gaze, and she couldn't for the life of her tear it away from him. "I will wait until you are ready, but I will never let you go. You are my mate and some day you will accept me."

Her jaw dropped, and her mind threatened to spin out of control at his words. *Yes! No!* The words alternated in her mind as he closed the distance between them. Her eyes closed, and she expected to feel his lips on hers, but nothing happened.

"Fuck!"

Her eyes shot open when he swore. Staring at the floor, he shook his head slowly before abruptly getting to his feet and storming out of the kitchen.

She stared after him for several seconds before closing her eyes and leaning back against the cushions. What the hell had just happened? It was like she had entered a different reality, and her choices had been removed. The man she had taken to be gentle and patient, had just shown a completely different side of himself, and she didn't know how to feel about that.

Sabrina knew how she *should* feel about it. Leith talking about her like she was property should seriously piss her off and make her run screaming from this house and him. So, why was she feeling all hot and ready to throw caution to the wind and beg him to take her to bed? It was completely unacceptable and confusing, and made her question her own sanity.

Footsteps entering the kitchen had her slowly opening her eyes. Leith stopped in the middle of the room with an unreadable expression on his face. His stance gave the impression that he was relaxed, but the tension in his jaw told her he wasn't. "I'm sorry, my angel. I hope you can forgive my harsh words." He opened his mouth like he was going to continue, but then he closed it and turned away from her.

"Am I your mate?" Staring at the back of his head, she waited for him to answer her.

Several seconds went by before he did. "Yes, you are my mate. I wanted you to have time to get to know me before I told you. I have been waiting for you for a long time, and now that you are here, all I can think about is mating you and keeping you forever. But no matter how that sounds, I will never force you. You will take the time you need to accept me."

"And if I can't?" Keeping her eyes on him, she

waited for his reaction. He had yet to turn back to face her.

"I will wait and hope, my angel, and do everything I can to help you accept me." His shoulders sagged a little. "Do you not find me to your liking?" There was pain and maybe even fear in his voice as he asked the question.

Sabrina sat up and swung her legs to the floor to go to him. But as soon as her feet hit the floor, she was reminded why she was on the couch in the first place. Gasping, she clenched her fists to hold on until the pain subsided a little.

Leith was at her side in a heartbeat, gently chiding her for not being careful. He helped her move her legs back up onto the sofa before kneeling beside her on the floor. "Try to relax. I will get some ice for your leg. I should have done that earlier. Please forgive me."

Before she could respond, he stormed off again, leaving her alone. But at least this time she knew why he left and that he was going to be right back.

It only took a minute before he rushed back into the kitchen with something wrapped in a towel. "I am all out of ice in the freezer downstairs it seems, but I found a bag of frozen vegetables."

She burst out laughing as he unwrapped the towel to reveal a bag of frozen peas. He wrapped the towel once around her ankle, covered the injured area with the bag of peas, and wrapped the rest of the towel around it to keep it in place.

When he seemed satisfied that her ankle was taken care of, he turned to her with a solemn expression on his face. "My angel, I—"

"You're up early." Julianne's cheerful voice

sounded from the entrance to the kitchen. "What are you... Oh no, what happened?" Her friend stared at her leg before meeting Sabrina's gaze.

"Just a sprained ankle." Sabrina smiled. "Nothing to worry about. I didn't expect to see you this early in the morning."

"I..." Moving her gaze to Leith, Julianne stopped before obviously changing what she had been about to say. "We can't stay in bed all day just because we're mated. Besides, we have a witch to catch."

Sabrina felt herself frowning as she realized she had completely forgotten about Ambrosia. The morning had been spent with Leith, and apparently, her brain hadn't been able to focus on anything else.

"How did you manage to twist your ankle?" Julianne had walked up to the couch and was studying Sabrina's leg with a concerned expression.

"A rock rolled away from under my foot as I stepped on it, walking back from the beach after watching the sunrise. I should've paid better attention to where I was going." She sighed. "If Leith hadn't been there to help me, I would've had to crawl back to the house." As she spoke, she swung her gaze up to the attractive man standing quietly next to her.

He met her gaze and gave her a short nod of acknowledgement. "Would you ladies like some coffee? I think I need some caffeine."

"Thank you, Leith. Coffee would be perfect right now." Sabrina smiled up at him.

"Oh, yes please, thank you." Julianne's smile lit up her face, and she went to take a seat on the other sofa. "Would you mind making some for Duncan as well? He'll be here in a minute."

"Of course." Leith turned and walked over to the coffee machine.

Julianne's eyes filled with amusement as her gaze swung back to Sabrina. "So, I take it you weren't skinny-dipping then if the sun was coming up."

The sound of something crashing to the floor by the coffee machine startled her, and Sabrina's gaze shot to Leith, who was staring back at her with his jaw slack and eyes starting to glow emerald.

Julianne's laughter helped Sabrina tear her gaze away from his. Taking a deep breath to try to prevent herself from blushing, she narrowed her eyes at her friend. "Not amusing."

"Yes, it was." Julianne nodded vigorously with a wicked grin on her face.

"What's amusing but not?" Duncan strode into the kitchen and aimed directly for Julianne.

"Just teasing Sabrina. Sorry, Sabrina, I couldn't help myself. It was too easy." Her friend rose and closed the distance to her mate. "I missed you, big boy."

Sabrina couldn't help rolling her eyes as Julianne and Duncan practically devoured each other right in front of her. She was quickly learning what Duncan had meant when he had spoken of newly mated couples with amusement in his voice. They could hardly keep their hands off each other, let alone be in separate places for longer than a minute or two. It was both disturbing and fascinating.

Seeing that kind of love between two people was amazing, but Sabrina wasn't sure she wanted something that all-consuming for herself. It seemed exhausting to be that engrossed in, and dependent on, someone else. And the fact that this might be what

Leith expected of her if she mated him scared her. But then she didn't have to worry about that since she would never be able to be his mate.

She winced and rubbed her chest as her heart chose that moment to act up. Sinking back against the cushions, she closed her eyes and took several slow, deep breaths to try to settle her racing heart. She'd had atrial fibrillation since her early teens, but since it didn't happen frequently and never lasted more than a few minutes, she had never sought medical treatment for the condition.

A hand on her shoulder startled her, and her eyes popped open to stare up into dark-green orbs made even darker by the concern in them. "Are you in pain? Can I get you some painkillers? I think I have some somewhere."

Giving him a weak smile, she shook her head. "No, I'll be fine in a minute. Thank you, Leith."

He studied her face with a frown on his face, apparently not sure she was speaking the truth. "You look pale, and your heart is racing. Perhaps I should call a doctor."

"Leith, this happens to me occasionally. It's nothing to worry about. Just give me a couple of minutes." Focusing on making her smile confident, she held his gaze.

"I don't like it." Kneeling on the floor next to her, he put a hand on her forehead like he was checking for a fever.

And just like that her heart settled back into a normal rhythm, and she breathed out a sigh of relief.

CHAPTER 3

"How often does this happen, my angel?" Leith tried to keep the worry out of his voice as he questioned her. If she had a heart condition, it just increased the urgency of them mating. No matter what kind of illness she had, it would be cured as soon as they mated, and no disease of any kind would be able to touch her after that. That was one of the benefits of mating someone like him.

Her smile was soft, and he got the impression it was meant to be deliberately disarming to make sure he calmed and stopped asking more questions. "Just once or twice a week, and it only lasts for a few minutes each time. As I said, nothing to worry about."

He did worry, though. Human disease was something he was spared from, so he had no experience with it firsthand, but he had plenty of experience with seeing it destroy even the strongest humans. None of them had any real defense against it, even though the medical profession had come a long way in eradicating some illnesses. And death wasn't the worst consequence. It was the pain and suffering he hated the most.

Not wanting to push her, he rose to his feet and indicated the cup on the coffee table. "Enjoy your coffee, Sabrina. Is there anything else I can get you? Some food, perhaps?"

She smiled up at him. "Thank you, but I think I'd like to enjoy my coffee first."

"Of course." He picked up the cup and handed it to her, meeting her beautiful blue gaze as he did. "Just tell me when you are ready to eat, my angel, and I will make whatever you desire."

The last word he uttered had his thoughts reverting to Julianne's comment a few minutes ago. As he headed back to the coffee machine, an image of Sabrina swimming naked in the loch lodged in his mind. He had never seen her naked, but he could only imagine she would be stunning without clothes covering her body. His cock hardened, and his hands practically itched to touch her, and there was no doubt his eyes were shining like green beacons announcing his desire.

Without breaking his stride, Leith quickly changed direction and headed out of the kitchen before continuing out the front door. He could hardly remember the last time a woman had turned him on like this. It had been many years ago, and it had taken a lot more than just the thought of her naked to get him this revved up.

But Sabrina wasn't just any woman; she was his mate. And he was coming to realize that even three hundred years of experience hadn't prepared him for the power his mate wielded over his mind and body. He had watched mates drive each other crazy with lust and jealousy more than once in his lifetime, but he had never thought it would apply to him. Being more powerful than most shifters, he had considered himself above such baser feelings, but he had been wrong. And with Sabrina's reluctance to accept him and his lack of readiness for that situation, he had a feeling he had barely scratched the surface of what it meant to pine for your mate.

Taking a deep breath, he focused on what to do next. Sabrina needed his help while her leg healed, and he was going to be there to take care of her every need. Her well-being was going to be his primary focus. Nothing else.

∞∞∞∞

All the people staying at Leith's house were gathered around the kitchen table for breakfast. Trevor and Jennie, Michael and Steph, and Duncan and Julianne. As well as Sabrina and himself.

Leith kept an eye on Sabrina as she ate. He had made sure she was seated at the end of the table with enough room for a second chair to rest her injured leg upon. And he was sitting directly to her left in case she needed anything.

"Okay, to sum up our plan." Trevor's deep voice broke through the chatter around the table. The big wolf shifter was seated across from Leith. "We need to pay a visit to some of the larger clans and packs to explain the situation with Ambrosia and discuss the fact that she's no longer just targeting alphas. Any unmated shifter, and particularly someone who has a score to settle or want to dominate, might be susceptible to her offer of power."

"And." Duncan chimed in from the other end of the table. "I've talked to Callum. He's on his way and will be here in about an hour to join us in our search. For those of you who haven't met him, he's a young wolf from Fearolc specializing in security systems. A gadget nerd in the best possible meaning and a great guy."

Michael chuckled where he was sitting next to Steph, his mate and a powerful witch who only recently discovered what she was. "Too bad Carlos isn't here. By the sounds of it, Carlos and Callum would have a lot to talk about."

Duncan nodded. "Yes, I imagine they would. Are James and Carlos and their wives still in Edinburgh, or have they left by now?"

Michael took Steph's hand in his and turned to smile at her. "They're leaving in a few hours. We'll be staying in Scotland for at least another week before we go to America to visit my family. Where we'll stay after that we haven't decided yet."

Steph's face stiffened a bit at the mention of America. "I can't say I'm looking forward to it. Your father sounds like a dick to be honest."

Michael burst out laughing with love shining in his eyes as he kept his gaze on his mate. "Oh, he is. A total dick. But you're the strongest woman I know. Seeing you take care of Jack proved to me that you can handle my father. And if you have to singe his skin a little to gain his respect, that's fine by me. I'll be right beside you, cheering you on. He deserves to be put in his place. And if a woman does it, all the better."

"You'll be fine, Steph." Jennie smiled at the other woman from across the table. "I'm new to all this witchy stuff, but I don't think many can go up against you and win."

"Thank you, Jennie." Steph gave her a small smile. "But this is Michael's father we're talking about. I don't really relish burning him to a crisp. He might be a dick, but few people deserve something like that."

"I can help you gain more control of your powers before you leave." Sabrina's voice caused Leith to turn to look at her. "We can practice somewhere safe where we can't hurt anyone."

Steph's face lit up. "That would be perfect, Sabrina. I would feel so much better if I knew I had some semblance of control."

"Control is vital." Sabrina smiled at the other witch. "Particularly with your level of power. But you already seem to have some control. The only person you have hurt before is Jack, am I right?"

"Yes." Steph nodded. "But I've never had that kind of explosive ability before, so—"

"Yes, you have," Sabrina stated firmly. "It's been inside you at least since your teens. What is unusual is that you didn't discover it earlier, but I'm guessing that's because you already had the ability to turn your powers on and off at will. You mentioned last night that you have been able to heal since you were a child. But you've consciously chosen when to use that ability, yes?"

Steph nodded again. "Yes, I realized at a young age that what I could do wasn't normal. After telling a few other kids and having them laugh at me and call me a liar, I made sure never to tell anyone else what I could do. Well, except an ex who hurt his hand. And he ended up wanting to use my healing power to get rich, and that was the end of that relationship."

"That's one of the reasons it's better to keep our extraordinary abilities to ourselves." The sadness in Sabrina's eyes had Leith wanting to pull her close and comfort her, but instead he took a sip of his orange juice.

"I know." Steph looked at Sabrina. "I really wish you would've let me heal your leg before breakfast."

Smiling, Sabrina shook her head. "No, there was no reason to make everyone wait to have breakfast. It's not that painful as long as I don't move my foot around or put any weight on it."

"Okay, but we'll fix that ankle as soon as we're done eating." Steph narrowed her eyes at Sabrina, clearly indicating this wasn't open for discussion. Then, she let her gaze travel around the table, a smile spreading across her face. "It's fantastic not having to hide who I am all the time. With you I can be myself. Thank you all so much." She stopped when she met Michael's gaze. "And you most of all, my true mate. I can't believe my luck in finding you."

Michael chuckled. "To be fair I was the one who found you, remember?"

Leith averted his eyes when Michael leaned toward Steph, clearly intending to kiss her. It reminded him of how close he had been to kissing Sabrina earlier that morning. He hadn't realized that she had hurt her leg when he pulled her into his arms. He had just acted on instinct when he noticed her falling. But when their gazes met, his body had taken over, and he bent his head slowly toward her until she screamed in pain and sagged against him.

"Can you pass me the juice please, Leith?" Sabrina's question ripped him out of his thoughts and made him turn to her.

"Of course, my angel." He picked up the juice and refilled her glass before raising his gaze to hers. "Anything else I can get you?"

The corners of her lips curved upward in a small smile as she met his gaze. "No, thank you."

He gave her a short nod, before turning to Trevor. "You're going to talk to the shifter groups out east?"

"Yes." Trevor glanced at Jennie before turning back to Leith. "It might take us a couple of days to talk to all three groups, so we'll be staying in Aberdeen for at least one night if not two. Duncan and Julianne were talking about going to Glasgow and visiting the pack just north of Perth on the way there. Did she mention it to you yet?" Trevor swung his gaze to Sabrina. "I think she wanted you to join them."

Leith's lungs seized, or at least that was how it felt. Just the thought of her leaving made him want to grab her, hold her tightly, and scream *mine*. Much like a two-year-old with a new toy. He glanced down the table to where Duncan and Julianne were sitting. They were talking and clearly hadn't heard Trevor mentioning them.

"She hasn't mentioned it yet, but I'm sure she will." Sabrina frowned and continued in a low voice. "I think I might pass, though, and let the new mates enjoy some time alone together."

Leith breathed a silent sigh of relief. But apparently, it was too soon.

"Maybe I should go to Edinburgh. I have family there that I can stay with. I'm not going to be much help here, anyway, while you're all away talking to the various shifter groups."

"No, I need you here." Leith stared at her and saw her eyes widen in shock. Realizing what he had just said, he silently swore. He was going to drive her away with his possessive behavior. "I mean I would appreciate your help in our search for Ambrosia. You are the most experienced witch we know, and you will be invaluable when we find her. And hopefully that will be soon. I was going to offer to go up north to talk to the packs and clans located in that area, and I was hoping that you would agree to come with me."

Sabrina's jaw tensed and she stared at him. "I um… Perhaps that's not—"

"Please, my angel." Leith held her gaze. "We need to catch Ambrosia before she causes irreparable damage to the shifter community, not to mention humanity who have no defense at all against someone like her." It was all true, but he was aware he was using the situation with Ambrosia to make sure Sabrina agreed to join him. Not entirely honorable, but he couldn't bear the thought of her leaving. Leith wasn't even sure he would be able to let her leave if she tried, and he didn't want to think about what that said about him as a person.

Sabrina broke their eye contact and looked at her plate. "Well, when you put it like that it's kind of hard to refuse."

"Does that mean you're coming with me?" Leith didn't look away from her face.

Nodding slowly, she raised her gaze to his. "I'll

come with you."

CHAPTER 4

Shit, shit, shit! Sabrina should have come up with an excuse to leave, but being put on the spot like that, she hadn't been able to come up with a good explanation for why she didn't want to help. And Leith was right that Ambrosia was dangerous and needed to be stopped. It just wasn't safe for Sabrina to be around this man. Not safe for her sanity or for her control, which meant that it wasn't safe for other people either. If she was to lose control around these people... No, that couldn't happen. It was that simple.

"Thank you." The corner of Leith's mouth pulled up before he averted his eyes. Focusing on his orange juice, he grabbed his glass and sipped. It almost seemed like he was feeling bad for persuading her.

They finished their breakfast, and afterward the men cleared the table while the women headed over to the sofas by the window.

Sabrina declined Leith's offer to carry her to the couch. Instead, she let Steph support her while she hopped on one leg across the floor. They sat down on one of the couches.

"Okay, it's going to tingle a little, but there will be no pain." Steph smiled and placed Sabrina's leg on her lap.

"Sounds good." Sabrina returned Steph's smile and leaned back against the cushions to relax.

It felt exactly like Steph had said it would. As soon as the other woman put her hands on Sabrina's leg, a tingling sensation started and penetrated her ankle. Sabrina was surprised at how the healing energy specifically targeted the injury and didn't seem to spread farther up her leg or down to her toes.

Sabrina studied Steph's face. The woman's eyes were closed and from the tight expression on her face, there was no doubt Steph was concentrating hard on what she was doing. It was obvious to Sabrina that the other woman had a lot more control of her powers than she herself realized. Which meant that their training would be more about Steph exploring her abilities and understanding what she could do than actually gaining control of her abilities. Steph's control was already admirable.

Less than five minutes later, Steph opened her eyes and smiled. "Your leg should be fine now, but try using it and see how it feels."

"Thank you, Steph." Sabrina put her feet on the floor and carefully stood. She took a few steps away from the sofa before turning around. "That's amazing. It seems fully healed. There's no pain whatsoever. Thank you so much, for the healing and the experience. I've never had someone heal me before."

Shrugging like it was nothing, Steph smiled. "My

pleasure. It's fantastic to be able to use my ability to help people without worrying about there being consequences. Before I met Michael, I had pretty much resigned myself to never using my healing ability again."

∞∞∞

Sabrina was pacing in her room. As soon as Duncan and Julianne left, she had excused herself to go pack her things. Leith and Sabrina were going to visit at least three or four shifter groups up north, and one of them was tucked away somewhere remote, quite a few miles north of Inverness. They would probably be gone at least a couple of days.

It was close to two hours since Duncan and Julianne had left, taking Callum with them to visit a few shifter groups down south. Trevor and Jennie had left not long after breakfast, and Michael and Steph had decided to join them.

Callum had arrived about an hour after breakfast, and he had said he could work in the car while Duncan was driving. What he meant by work Sabrina didn't really know other than he had some ideas for tracking and locating people who didn't want to be found. But since they didn't know the true identity of Ambrosia, he was probably in for a challenge.

Sabrina stopped and stared at her bag. It had only taken her a few minutes to pack. So the truth was that the only reason Sabrina was still in her room was because she was hiding from the man of the house. Being alone with Leith in a car traveling north would be fine, but being alone with him in this house was totally different. It was more intimate somehow. Leith was an amazing man, pleasant and caring. And he would have been easy to talk to if she wasn't constantly aware of how attractive he was and how much she wanted to forget about the consequences and just be with him. But that wasn't a possibility.

The incident that happened when she was sixteen surfaced again, but she quickly pushed it to the back of her mind. Sabrina wasn't going to let Leith close enough for that to be an issue.

She had stayed in her room for way too long, but in her defense, Leith had told her they wouldn't be leaving until later in the day. He had a few things he needed to take care of first, and he wanted to call the alpha of each shifter group they were going to visit to make sure they were available and prepared when Leith and Sabrina arrived. Leith knew most of the alphas well, so he didn't expect there to be any trouble, but seeing as these were important discussions, he wanted to make sure they knew what to expect.

Pulling in a deep breath to center herself, Sabrina grabbed her bag. She let her eyes do a quick scan of the room to make sure nothing was out of place or forgotten before opening the door and stepping into the hallway. Only to come to an abrupt stop as she almost collided with Leith.

"Oh, I'm sorry." Tipping her head back, she let her eyes meet his dark-green orbs. The frown on his face made her take a step back away from him. He didn't look angry exactly, but more disappointed or even hurt.

"I am sorry, Sabrina. I think I have done you wrong. It was never my intention, but in doing so I have pushed you away from me." Leith sank down on one knee in front of her, and Sabrina felt her eyes round in shock as she backed up another step. The bag slipped from her hand and landed on the floor with a thud.

"Please accept my sincerest apologies, my angel." Keeping his gaze locked with hers, Leith took her right hand gently in his and brought it to his mouth. His warm lips touched her knuckles lightly, and she shuddered as heat raced through her body at his touch.

"I… Sure." She nodded slowly. "But what exactly have you done? I'm not sure I understand."

"I played on your conscience to make you stay with me, instead of being honest with you about how I feel and what I want. You deserve better than that, Sabrina, and I will not stop you if you choose to leave. If you still want to go to Edinburgh, I can drive you there myself, or if you would rather take the train, I can take you to Fort William or Inverness depending on your preference."

Sabrina stared at him, taking in the sadness in his eyes. She opened her mouth to respond to his offer, only to close it again when she realized she didn't know what to say. There was no doubt that the safest choice would be to take him up on his offer to drive her to the train station, but the thought of never seeing him again was preventing her from uttering the words. She didn't want to leave, even though she knew it was for the best. And he might have used Ambrosia's evil plan as an excuse to make her agree to stay, but that didn't make the evil witch's plan any less dangerous. Ambrosia had to be found and dealt with, and Sabrina could help with that.

"I will help you in your search for Ambrosia, Leith. It's important to stop her. But I only have another week of vacation left, so if it takes longer than that I will have to do what I can from London." She watched the relief in his eyes at her words. It would give them more time to get to know each other, and she was inwardly relishing that fact, even though she should be focusing on keeping him at a safe distance.

"Thank you, my angel." He rose, and a small smile curved his lips.

Sabrina felt her jaw drop, completely taken by surprise by his smile. Because even though he wasn't giving her a big grin, it was a smile, an expression she hadn't yet seen on his face. And although she had thought him handsome before, his smile pushed his level of attractiveness up to gorgeous. Easily. And not in an angelic kind of way, either, but in a bad boy dressed up as a nice guy kind of way. It was rattling, and completely detrimental to her motivation to stay away from him.

"I…" She swallowed and tried again. "You should smile more often." It wasn't what she had intended to say. Heat suffused her face, and she tore her gaze away from his.

"If that is your wish, I will." He tugged slightly on her hand, making her realize he was still holding onto it. "Are you ready to go? I have booked us a hotel room in Inverness. First thing tomorrow we will visit the panther clan located just east of the city. Today, I would like to take you on a tour of the city before we have dinner at a small restaurant I like. Does that sound okay with you?"

"Yes." She raised her gaze to his again. "That

sounds... nice. I'm packed and ready, so we can leave whenever you want."

His smile widened and turned more wicked, and Sabrina almost groaned out loud in response. She had struggled with her attraction to him when he looked all solemn. The way he was smiling at her at the moment was threatening to turn her knees to jelly and heat her core until she had to find somewhere away from people where she could do something to alleviate her need.

"Then let us go." Leith suddenly bent and picked up her bag before turning away from her and striding toward the stairs.

Taking a deep breath to try to calm her mind and body, she followed him upstairs and out the front door. A sleek black sports car was parked right outside the door, and when he opened the trunk, she noticed his bag was already inside.

Sabrina got into the passenger seat of the powerful vehicle. What was it with shifters and horsepower? The ones she had met all drove a sports car. Well, except Michael, but his was a rental so that didn't count.

Leith got in and they took off. After rounding the southern end of Loch Ness, they sped north along the western side of the loch. Sabrina hadn't paid attention to the speed limit, but they must have been breaking it the way Leith was driving. At this rate they would reach Inverness in no time.

***

Leith kept his eyes on where they were going while speeding along the familiar road. He knew the area intimately, having lived in practically the same location for more than three hundred years. And although there had been changes over the years like the introduction of cars and paved roads, the area wasn't all that different from when he was a boy.

Steeling himself for the conversation he was about to launch into, he glanced at the beautiful woman sitting beside him. He had known whom she was the moment he had first laid eyes on her. Not by appearance but by her power signature. It had immediately called to him, telling him exactly whom she was. His mate. The woman he had been hoping to find for more than two hundred years.

"Are you comfortable, my angel?"

Sabrina nodded. "Yes. Do all shifters love sports cars? I know many humans do, but that almost seems more natural, since they don't have any superpowers and instead have to buy power and speed."

"I believe most shifters do. We have a love of speed and power as well, and we usually have money that we have amassed throughout our long lives."

"I guess that makes sense." Sabrina glanced at him. "Do you usually drive this fast?"

He shrugged. "I can slow down if it makes you uncomfortable. But this is how I usually drive, yes. This car is built for speed, and I enjoy it."

"No." Sabrina shook her head. "It's okay. You seem to be in control."

Without any more hesitation, he dived into what he wanted to say. "I want to talk to you about something, Sabrina. It might be unfair to you to do this now while we are in a car and you cannot escape, but it is important to me to be able to say this, and I hope you will listen to me for a little while." He glanced at her.

"You are my mate, but I did not intend to tell you that so soon. I wanted you to get to know me before I told you. But now that you know, I sense that you do not approve of me or return my feelings."

Sabrina turned her head to stare at him for several seconds before she said anything. "How can you talk about feelings so soon? We just met yesterday."

"I have been waiting for you for more than two hundred years, my angel. And it might seem strange to you that I already have feelings for you, but a lot of shifters know at once when they meet their mates, if they are lucky enough to do so. We do not need time for feelings to develop as we get to know each other. The bond is there from the time we meet and even before the act of mating. The act solidifies the mating bond further and is important for a solid relationship, but we feel drawn to the person before that."

Shaking her head slowly, Sabrina turned away from him. "I can't be your mate, Leith, and it's not because I don't like you or don't approve of you. I'll never be able to give you all you need and deserve."

Leith felt himself frowning at her choice of words. "What is it that you believe you cannot give me?"

"I…" She hesitated, squirming in her seat. "I don't really want to talk about this. Please just take my word for it that I can't be your mate. You'd be better off choosing someone else."

His hands tightened on the wheel as his whole body tensed with agitation. "That is just it, Sabrina. I do not have a choice. You are my mate. There is no changing that fact. A shifter only has one true mate, and once we meet that person, it is damn near impossible to walk away. If I had never met you, I might have been able to mate someone else. It would not have been a perfect mating, but it would have been good. But that is not an option anymore. You are my mate, my one true and only mate. No one else will ever catch my eye again."

The silence stretched between them when he closed his mouth, an awkward silence that felt anything but good.

"Then I regret meeting you." Her words were so soft they were barely audible, but their impact was like being hit by a truck and had him swerving into the other lane before he regained control of the car and slowed down.

Leith's heart raced like he had just slashed the world record in the four hundred meters hurdles in half. And it wasn't from losing control of the car. His true mate didn't want him. She even regretted meeting him. The one thing he had always wanted and hoped for had just crashed and burned at his feet.

He slowed down and turned off onto a small gravel road. After driving about a hundred yards, he stopped the car and just sat there staring ahead without seeing anything of what was in front of him.

"Leith?" Sabrina's quiet voice penetrated his turbulent thoughts, and he felt himself frowning. "Why have we stopped?"

He swallowed hard and squeezed his eyes shut. "Because I need a minute before I can continue driving. I cannot focus right now. It is not safe. I am sorry."

CHAPTER 5

Sabrina stared at the beautiful man beside her, not sure what to say or do. One minute he seemed to be taken by her as a person, even acting like he was developing romantic feelings for her. And the next he was all business, stating that she was his mate like neither of them had a choice in the matter, and it was just a transaction that needed to happen. She wanted to shout at him and comfort him all at the same time. But at the end of the day, it didn't matter what he did or didn't feel. She couldn't agree to be his mate.

Taking a deep breath, she turned away from him. This was so different from the feelings she had watched develop between Julianne and Duncan. It had happened extremely fast, too fast really, but it had been genuine. The two of them hadn't been able to stay away from each other, their feelings and sexual attraction pulling them together like two powerful magnets.

Whatever was driving Leith to mate her was clearly

different, and perhaps it had something to do with the kind of shifter he was. He didn't want to tell her, and in that as well he was different from the other shifters she had met so far. They weren't hiding what they were like he was.

"Sabrina." Leith saying her name interrupted her thoughts, and she turned her head to look at him. "I will drive you to the train station in Inverness. From there you can catch the train to Edinburgh, and onward to London if that is your wish. I do not think I will be able to spend time with you knowing that you do not want to be with me. It will be too painful."

Painful. It wasn't a word she had expected him to use, and the way he said it, it almost sounded like he had feelings for her after all. Like she wasn't just the person he needed to mate, but someone who meant something to him. Maybe she was stupid or something, but his mixed signals were messing with her mind and her perception of him and his personality. And that was unusual for her. She couldn't seem to get a good grasp of what this man was really like and how he felt. It was unnerving.

"I think it might be best for me to leave, but what do you mean by painful?" She forced herself to hold his gaze. "Are you talking about physical pain because of the mating bond, or are you talking about emotions?"

"I am not sure I can separate the two." He sighed. "It is both an emotional and physical pain. Perhaps one day I will be able to think back and describe it more eloquently and objectively, but right now it just feels like my beating heart has been ripped from my body."

Sabrina gasped, and she hunched forward as pain like she had never felt before slammed into her chest, ripping and tearing at her heart like it was being shredded into small pieces.

"Sabrina?" A hand landed on her back, and just like that the pain was gone. "Are you in pain? What can I do?"

Shaking her head, she spoke through her heavy breathing. "I'm okay. I don't know what that was. I've never felt anything like it."

"What did it feel like?" Leith's hand was sliding soothingly up and down her back.

Her breathing was starting to settle, and she turned to him. His eyes were filled with concern, and he studied her face like he was trying to find the answer to his question in her expression. "Like my heart was being torn to pieces."

His eyes narrowed. "And that's never happened before? Not even anything similar?"

"No." She shook her head slowly. "Never."

"I am taking you to the hospital." Leith started the car and put it in reverse.

"I don't think that's necessary." She tried to meet his eyes, but his focus was on his mirrors as he reversed toward the main road. "Leith."

"It is necessary. I can accept that you do not want me, but I cannot watch you die. So do not ask me to." His features were set in a determined expression as he backed out onto the road after making sure there was no traffic.

Sabrina could only stare at him. His concern seemed a bit excessive. One episode of chest pain most likely didn't mean anything. If it had persisted, then yes, but it only lasted for a few seconds. She doubted the hospital would do more than take her blood pressure before sending her away with the advice to come back if the pain returned. Anyway, she wasn't going to the hospital. "I'm not going to die. That's a bit extreme."

"Yes, you are." He stared straight ahead as they sped toward Inverness. "But not yet. I won't allow it."

She wasn't sure how to respond to that. The solemn, easygoing man she had met the day before had changed into a stubborn, high-handed individual overnight. It was, of course, too soon to think that you knew someone after one day, but she usually had a person correctly pegged just a few minutes after meeting them, so having someone take her by surprise like this was rattling.

To be fair he was concerned for her health at the moment, and that explained his current determination and harsh words. But it didn't help her decide how to respond to him.

∞∞∞∞

They drove in silence until they entered the city of Inverness. Leith had several times started to say something only to stop himself. He had never considered that his mate wouldn't accept him. It was a situation he was completely unprepared for, and the emotional impact was preventing him from thinking clearly and coming up with a plan for how to handle this. The mating bond always affected both parties; it was never a one-way thing. Not even when one of the parties was human. So, Sabrina should be feeling a pull toward him just like he was feeling a pull toward her. And it would only get worse the longer they went without mating.

Unless her being a witch altered that somehow. He had never come across the combination witch and shifter before Michael and Steph, and he hadn't asked them about their experiences. Maybe he should have. But what happened to them at the hands of Jack and Ambrosia might have overshadowed any influence the bond had on Steph. She might not have noticed it at all with everything that happened to the couple.

He found a spot and parked outside the main hospital. Being a shifter, he had never needed to go to one before, and it felt strange to be heading into a place where humans were frequently dying from disease or injury. He had survived a lot of humans throughout the years, obviously, but he had never visited someone in a hospital. Not a modern one, at least. Just the thought of entering such a place left him cold.

"Leith, I don't need—"

"Please." He turned to the beautiful woman he wanted more than life itself. "Indulge me. I just want to make sure there is nothing seriously wrong with you."

Sabrina sighed and met his gaze. "I realize that, but I can't go in there. If they decide to take my blood, they'll find an anomaly, something that shouldn't be there."

"What do you mean?" Leith could feel himself frowning.

"I'm not sure exactly what it is. Nobody else in my family has ever had this issue, so it doesn't seem like it's related to me being a witch. But I don't know. After our local GP informed us of an anomaly in my bloodwork as a child, he wanted to run more tests. My mom refused, and she managed to get him to drop the whole thing. I don't know how, because he seemed really eager to study me.

"After a few years, we had my blood tested anonymously at a private facility, and they found the same thing. They practically begged to meet the person the blood belonged to, but we refused. It was all handled by our family solicitor, so our names were never mentioned. We received their report, but it didn't tell us anything useful since they didn't know what the anomaly meant. But they wanted us to confirm that the blood was taken from a person who was still alive. We didn't respond to that, of course."

Leith didn't know what to say. Sabrina had a good reason not to seek medical help, the same reason he had, in fact, being a shifter and not human. The difference was that he didn't need medical help with his healing capabilities, but Sabrina did. "We will call Michael and Steph and have them meet us halfway between here and wherever they are at the moment. Steph can heal you if there is something that needs healing."

Sabrina gave him a small smile, but it didn't reach her eyes. "I don't think so. Healing someone's heart is considered high risk. My mom is a good healer, but she never tries to heal someone's heart or head. If something goes wrong, the consequences are too severe. That's an accepted truth among the witches in my family."

He wanted to argue that truth, based on the simple

fact that it was better to be alive than dead. But how could he? It wasn't his place to question the knowledge witches had developed over generations.

Leith turned away and stared out of the window at the busy entrance of the hospital. If only Sabrina would accept him, her health would no longer be an issue. But it was her choice, and he couldn't pressure her to like him. Not even for health reasons like this. Just mentioning it as a possible cure felt like a form of manipulation, and he wouldn't do that.

But there was one thing he couldn't do no matter how much it was going to hurt to spend time with her when she clearly didn't want him. He couldn't let her go off alone back to London when there was a risk she might have another episode on the train. At the very least he wanted to observe her condition for a few days to make sure he was available to deal with any recurrence of the pain she experienced earlier.

"Leith?" Sabrina's voice was soft when she said his name.

Taking a deep breath, he pasted a smile on his face before turning back to her. "Yes, my angel."

"Can we go to the hotel now, please? I think I need to lie down for a little while." She looked tired, and Leith felt his whole body tense with apprehension.

"What's wrong?" He studied her face. "Are you in pain again?"

"No. Well, yes, but not like before. Just a headache. I get them now and then, but it usually helps to rest in a quiet, dark room for a little while." The corners of her lips curved slightly like she was trying to give him a reassuring smile, but she didn't quite succeed.

"Okay." He started the engine and carefully pulled

out from the parking spot. "The hotel is only a few minutes away. Close your eyes and try to relax until we get there."

Leith focused on driving smoothly through the streets of Inverness, to avoid any unnecessary bumps and jolts that would cause Sabrina more pain than she was already experiencing. More pain. Fury like he hadn't felt in decades surged through his body. It was unacceptable. His mate shouldn't have to experience pain.

After pulling up in front of the private entrance to the hotel, he quickly exited the car and hurried around to the passenger side. He allowed Sabrina to get out of the car before scooping her up in his arms.

Her eyes widened as she stared up at him. "I can—"

"No!" The word came out harder than he had intended, and he softened his voice before continuing. "I am carrying you to our suite. No discussion." He turned and started toward the hotel entrance just as a hotel employee opened the door.

"Our suite?" Her eyes seemed to grow even bigger.

"Yes." Leith swung his gaze to the man holding the door open for them. "Please bring the luggage up to our suite and park the car."

The man nodded. "Certainly, sir."

"Thank you." Leith walked past the man and headed for the stairs. Sabrina's head sagged against his chest, and a small whimper escaped her lips as he started ascending the stairs two steps at a time. Silently swearing at himself for not being careful enough, he slowed his pace to make their ascent as comfortable for her as possible.

The door to the suite opened when they approached, and another hotel employee greeted them and held the door while Leith carried Sabrina into the suite. Then, the door closed behind them, and they were left alone.

Leith didn't stop but continued into the large bedroom containing a massive bed. She opened her eyes when he gently lowered her down onto the soft mattress. "Is there anything I can do for you, my angel? Anything that will soothe your pain?"

Her gaze met his. "If you can please close the curtains. And there are some painkillers in my bag. Two tablets with a glass of water would be perfect."

He gave her a short nod before quickly striding over to the window and yanking the curtains shut, making sure they were properly closed before moving into the other room.

Leith was just evaluating whether to get their bags himself when there was a knock on the door. He opened the door and thanked the man standing there before taking the bags from him.

There was no time to carefully search through Sabrina's bag; instead, he emptied the entire contents out onto the large sofa. After grabbing the small bottle of pain meds, he picked up a glass of water from the bar area before heading back into the bedroom.

The sight that met him made his anger spike again. She looked so small and defenseless curled up on her side on the large bed, her face almost as pale as the crisp white linen.

Useless. That's how he felt. Completely useless in the face of her pain. And he abhorred that feeling more than anything.

He put the glass of water on the bedside table before removing two tablets from the bottle. "Sabrina, would you like some help sitting up?"

"Yes, please." Her voice was weak, and she didn't even open her eyes to look at him. But she rolled slowly over onto her back.

Lifting her upper body gently, he kept his gaze on her face to judge her reaction to the movement. When she didn't show any signs of increased discomfort, he used some of the large pillows to support her back and head. "I have your painkillers and a glass of water." He opened her right hand and put the two tablets in her cold and clammy palm.

She slowly cracked open her eyes. Holding his gaze, she put the pills in her mouth before reaching for the glass.

He handed her the glass of water and watched her down half of its content before handing the glass back to him.

"Thank you, Leith." Her eyes fell shut. "I'll just rest until those start working. They won't eliminate the pain, but they'll reduce it enough for the nausea to stop, and I'll be able to relax and move around. And that in turn usually helps to remove the pain completely."

"Do you want me to remove the pillows so you can lie down again?" He could feel himself frowning as he stared at her pale face. *Able to move around.* He inwardly swore. He wanted the pain gone completely, not just reduced enough to be bearable. This was one of the reasons he didn't spend a lot of time with humans anymore. All their pain and suffering weren't something he wanted to bear witness to. He had done enough of that in his youth to last him a lifetime. A very long lifetime. And watching his mate in pain was significantly worse.

"Yes, that would be perfect." She tipped her head forward slightly but stopped abruptly and winced with obvious pain.

Leith had a sudden thought. "Are these headaches you are getting stress-related?"

"Tension headaches, yes." Sabrina didn't move her head this time or open her eyes. "That's what the neurologists believe, and I think they might be right."

He lifted her upper body gently and removed the pillows before lowering her body until she rested against the mattress. "Would you allow me to massage your neck and shoulders? If you do not want me to, I will respect that, but I believe it might help."

She took a deep breath before responding. "It sometimes helps, but you don't have to—"

"Of course I do. Why did you not tell me to do that at once? I will do anything—" Leith cut himself off when her body tensed, and a wince marred her beautiful face; he realized he had raised his voice. "I am so sorry, my angel. It will be my honor to give you a massage."

"Okay." The word was little more than a whisper as it crossed her stiff lips.

"Let me help you turn over."

After a little moving around, Sabrina was resting on her front with a large pillow supporting her upper body and chin. Leith was on his side beside her to avoid jolting her too much while giving her a massage. He would only be able to use one hand, but it was better than triggering her already nauseous stomach.

He watched her profile carefully as he started on her tense neck muscles. Using smooth yet firm movements, he slowly worked his way down her neck to the middle of her back before covering each of her shoulders. When he was done, he returned to her neck and started again. Gradually, her tense muscles relaxed and became supple beneath his fingers, and her breathing evened out in sleep.

Letting his hand rest on her back, he studied her profile. Color had returned to her cheeks, and she looked healthy again. It was all he could do not to pull her into his arms and lock her in a tight embrace forever. She was his, but for some reason, she didn't want to be.

Or perhaps that wasn't true. He frowned as he recalled what she had said in the car. *I can't be your mate, Leith, and it's not because I don't like you or don't approve of you. I'll never be able to give you all you need and deserve.*

But she had refused to tell him what she'd meant by that. And the only reason he could come up with for not wanting to tell him was that it was linked to some kind of trauma or incident she didn't want to remember or deal with.

Anger surged through him again. Maybe her rejection was all due to someone hurting her, causing her to see herself as unworthy of love and happiness. Or maybe it had something to do with her being a witch. It was impossible to say, but there was one thing he did know. He had to find the reason, and he was going to coax it out of her somehow.

Sabrina stirred beside him, and he studied her face to see if she was waking up. It had only been about half an hour since she swallowed the painkillers, and he hoped she would stay asleep until they started working. The massage seemed to have helped relax her muscles, but that didn't necessarily mean her headache was gone.

Leith started when she suddenly rolled onto her side, plastering her back against the front of his body. Her breathing was still even, and there was no indication she was awake. Not wanting to wake her, he didn't move or make a sound, but the feel of her so close was playing havoc with his body.

It didn't take long for his cock to harden where it was pressed against her ass, and he was left with a dilemma. Stay still to let her sleep, and risk her waking and feeling his erection? Or move away and risk her waking up with her head still hurting? He sighed and pulled away from her slowly. Rolling over onto his back, he made sure there was a distance of several inches between their bodies.

Leith stared up at the ceiling while willing his shaft to soften, but it clearly remembered the feel of Sabrina's soft ass with fondness and had no intention of forgetting it so soon. No surprise really. She was his mate, and his need to claim her as his was getting stronger. Being this close to her didn't exactly lessen that need.

Without warning, Sabrina rolled toward him and buried her head against his chest. Her left hand slid across his stomach before fisting his shirt above his right pec, pinching his nipple as she tightened her grip.

His dick twitched, and he couldn't prevent the groan that slipped from between his lips. Desire raced through him, and he had to concentrate not to crush her against him and capture her lips in a devouring kiss. He was trapped. There was no way he could pull away from her without waking her. But at least his erection wasn't pressed against her body at the moment. She had to actually move on top of him to feel it.

He swallowed the groan that forced its way up his throat at the image that had just lodged itself in his mind. Sabrina sitting on his cock was one hell of a visual. She would be magnificent.

Her hand let go of his shirt, and his nipple, and slowly slid down his stomach, causing his breath to seize in his lungs. He should stop her progress south, but he couldn't bring himself to do it. Whatever she did was on her, and he wanted her to touch him. Craved it more than his next breath.

He sucked in a breath as her hand reached his pants and continued over the hard ridge of his cock. Her palm pressed firmly against his swollen member, following it to the base before returning slowly toward the head.

"My angel." He groaned the endearment as his dick started throbbing. His balls were already pulled up tightly to his body as he anticipated glorious release.

CHAPTER 6

The feel of Leith's hard cock through the fabric of his pants was thrilling. And Sabrina was safe to explore him within the boundaries of her dream. It was the only place she could freely enjoy him. Hopefully, she would have a lot of dreams like this one, even after she left him to go back to her normal life.

She gave his thick shaft a light squeeze, and his whole body jerked. It made her chuckle with delight at how real the dream felt. Just like she was really there beside him. Even his scent was how she remembered. Salt and sea with a little spice that she couldn't identify. She loved his scent. It was an absolute turn-on.

Taking a deep breath, she turned her head and opened her eyes. Watching her hand stroking him through his pants, she marveled at his size. He was both longer and wider than any man she had ever been with. Not that she had been with a lot, but there had been a few. None of them measured up to Leith. She would have loved to try to take him inside her, and why not? It was her dream, and she could do whatever she wanted. Her channel clenched in response. She was already wet from the sheer thrill of caressing him. Grinning, she lifted her head from his chest and turned to look at him.

Emerald eyes were shining at her from beneath hooded eyelids, and the corners of his lips were pulled up in what could only be described as a sinful smile. "Sabrina." His voice was dark and rough, like it hadn't been used in days, and it flowed over her, making her shudder with lust. "You can do whatever you please with me. I am at your disposal."

Shock reverberated through her like she had just hit a rock wall at eighty miles an hour. Not a dream. This wasn't a dream at all. She backed off the bed so fast she ended up in a pile on the floor beside the bed. Her elbow took a hit in the fall, but whatever pain she was supposed to feel drowned in the shock she was experiencing. Her eyes felt like saucers, and her jaw was slack while she kept staring at Leith, not able to break their fused gazes.

Scrambling to get up, she finally managed to rip her eyes away from his. But before she could untangle her arms and legs, he was there gripping her hips and lifting her to her feet.

"Just relax, my angel. I don't expect—"

"No." The word was no more than a breath as she pushed his hands away from her and backed up several steps. He couldn't touch her, and she most definitely couldn't touch him. Her palm still remembered the feel of his hard length, but she had to forget that. Forget all about him and what could have been if things were different. If *she* were different.

She swallowed hard and kept her gaze on the floor at her feet. "I'm so sorry. I thought I was dreaming and was free to do whatever I want—" She cut off her explanation when she realized what she was saying. He wasn't supposed to know that she wanted him. It would be better for him if he didn't. That way he was free to find someone else without any regrets or concern for her feelings.

"So you want me then. That is not why you are trying to stay away from me." He took a step toward her, and Sabrina backed up.

Leith didn't stop, though, but continued moving toward her. Her back hit the wall, but he still kept coming until there was only a couple of inches separating their bodies. His hands flattened against the wall next to her shoulders, effectively trapping her. "I want to know why, Sabrina. And I will not accept any half-truths. I want all of it. Tell me." His voice was laced with anger.

Swallowing hard, she stared at his chest. His power was beating at her skin, at her body, but not in an unpleasant way. He was extremely good at hiding his immense power normally, but at the moment, he was letting it out to demonstrate his strength. Or perhaps it wasn't intentional at all, but rather a result of his anger.

"Sabrina." There was a definite warning in the way he said her name. "I will not let you go until you tell me."

"I..." She swallowed again, not sure how to start. He was right, though. It would be better if he knew. Then he would understand why she couldn't be all he wanted, and he would leave her alone. It would hurt, but she would just have to deal. Being around him was painful, so maybe it wouldn't be much worse than it already was.

"I've worked all my life to control my power." Tipping her head back, she forced herself to meet his emerald gaze. "Even before my power manifested itself in my teens, my mom trained me mentally to control it and educated me in the responsibility that follows having such power. I thought I was prepared when I started feeling it, but I wasn't." Her throat clogged, and she closed her eyes and just focused on her breathing for a few seconds until it passed. Opening her eyes, she met his gaze. His expression was unreadable, not giving her any clue as to what he was thinking. "I still don't have full control of my power, Leith. Whenever I get…worked up, I hurt anyone who's close to me."

She watched his expression change into one of horror as realization sank in. Closing her eyes, she let herself sag against the wall. Tears were filling her eyes, and she swallowed repeatedly to try to prevent them from falling. "I'm sorry," she whispered. Not that it made any difference, but it felt like something she should say. If she had been able to control her power, she could have been with this man. Been his mate and had a chance to make him happy. But that was impossible.

Sabrina expected him to pull away from her at any moment and tell her to leave. But several minutes went by and he was still standing in the same spot. And he hadn't said a word.

Slowly, she opened her eyes and tipped her head back to look up into his face. His eyes were no longer emerald but had changed back to their usual dark green. But the anger and disappointment she had expected to see in them wasn't there.

"Thank you for telling me, my angel. You should have told me sooner. Is that the only reason you refuse to be my mate?" There was careful hope in his expression and voice.

Nodding, she felt herself frowning. "Yes, but—"

"Good." A small smile curved his lips. "We will find a solution, my angel. I promise you. We have centuries ahead of us. And as long as I get to spend that time with you, I can handle anything. I would, of course, prefer to find the solution right this minute, but the important thing is that we are together."

"Centuries?" She was staring at him as her mind objected to his words. "But I'm—"

"Mine. You are mine." Emerald flashed in his eyes for a fraction of a second. "And when you become my mate, you will live as long as I do. It is common for all shifters. We cannot survive without our mates. Did Julianne not tell you this?"

Her mouth felt dry, and she couldn't find any words. *Centuries.* The word flashed like a neon sign in her mind.

"Come, my angel. I think you need to lie down." Leith's eyes were filled with concern when Sabrina met his gaze, and she realized her legs were wobbly, and she was holding onto his arms to be able to stay on her feet.

Without waiting for a response, he lifted her into his arms and carried her over to the bed.

"Leith." He stopped with her still in his arms, and she put a hand on his cheek. "Thank you for being so supportive, but I'm not sure—"

"I am." There wasn't an ounce of doubt in his eyes when he met her gaze. "You are mine, and I will take you however I can get you. Warts and all as they say, but I must say that you are remarkably wart free to be a witch. Perhaps they are all on your back. I guess I will find out in due time."

Sabrina burst out laughing. "I'll have you know that I have no warts like in the fairy tales."

His lips curved into a wicked smile. "So you say, but I reserve the right to check your whole body before I believe you. We will save that for another time, though."

Her jaw had gone slack at his statement. Just the thought of him exploring her body was enough to heat her blood with need. And being in his strong arms did nothing to diminish that need. She wanted to explore his body as well, and from what she had seen and felt so far, there was no doubt she would enjoy seeing him completely bared to her.

"We do have one pressing matter to attend to." His expression had sobered, but Sabrina's mind was still on his body.

"I take it you're not talking about your cock. Because that is one matter I can attend to." Smiling, she watched as his jaw slackened, and his eyes brightened. She wouldn't mind taking care of his needs, even though he couldn't take care of hers. Actually, she couldn't wait to take him into her mouth. Giving head was something she was good at, but it remained to be seen how well it would work with his larger size.

"No." The word was barely distinguishable from a growl, and he cleared his throat before he continued.

"As tempting as that sounds, I think we will postpone that until I can do something for you as well."

"Are you sure?" She narrowed her eyes at him. "Because that might be a long time."

His gaze dropped to her lips, and he gave her a short nod. "I am sure." Then he bent his head and brushed his lips briefly against hers before pulling back and staring at her. "The pressing matter I was talking about was food. We need something to eat. Hours have passed since we had breakfast, and I do not want my mate starving to death."

Sabrina snorted. "I admit I'm hungry but I'm in no danger of starving to death."

He turned away from the bed and carried her into the living room. "I do not want you to lose weight. That is all. Please don't take this the wrong way, but a woman is supposed to be soft. I am more than hard enough for the both of us."

Laughter burst from her lips. Not just because of his words but due to the serious expression on his face while he said them. "Yes, I agree. You're plenty hard enough."

He narrowed his eyes as his gaze met hers. "You are playing with fire, my angel. If you are not careful, I will take you somewhere far from people, so I can feel you lose control of your power as you come on my cock."

"No." An odd combination of need and horror raced through her at the scene Leith had just put in her mind, but horror soon took over as the scene ended with Leith in terrible pain. "I'll hurt you, and I'll never allow that."

"I sincerely doubt that. It takes a lot to hurt

someone like me." He didn't look the least bit concerned, and that increased her fear of hurting him.

"Leith, you don't know what I'm capable of." Staring into his eyes, she tried to convey her sincerity, but he didn't seem to take her seriously.

"And you have no idea how powerful I am, my angel."

CHAPTER 7

Leith smiled at the feel of Sabrina's hand in his as they strolled along the river Ness. It was late afternoon, and they had decided to explore the city after enjoying the food he had ordered for them.

There were still some obstacles they needed to face, but the most significant one was gone as far as he was concerned. She accepted him and wanted him, and that was all that mattered. It might take a few days before they were able to mate, but he was convinced that as long as he could get her alone without any people within striking distance, so to speak, he would be able to convince her to let him pleasure her. And it would prove to her that he could handle her power without any ill effects. He was much stronger than a normal shifter, but she didn't know that yet.

"I've never been to Inverness before. It's beautiful here." Her voice made him turn to her and meet her smile with his own.

"It is a city, and I must admit that I struggle to find

cities beautiful. I much prefer the countryside myself."

She chuckled. "I believe that, and the countryside suits you." Frowning, she averted her eyes. "For me I've always felt safer in the city. Less exposed in a way. It's easy to blend in and disappear among so many people. Much easier than in the countryside where everyone knows everybody else, and all you do and say get noticed." Cocking her head, she met his gaze. "How have you managed to stay in one place for so long without anyone noticing that you don't age and die?"

Leith wanted to ask her about her need to blend in and disappear, but instead he answered her question. "Unlike most shifters, I can change my appearance to look like I'm gradually aging. When the time is right, I pretend to die. Not literally in front of anyone, of course, but I have my young nephew come and take over the house and tell everyone that his uncle died."

"And the young nephew is you, just looking young again." A small smile curved her lips. "Sounds simple, but doesn't anyone ever get suspicious?"

"Occasionally there are questions, but none I cannot answer. I do not spend much time with humans, particularly not anyone living close by. It always complicates matters, and I learned long ago that it is better for someone like me to keep human friendships to a minimum. It means less difficulties and less pain. Humans die too easily." Leith took a deep breath and turned to stare straight ahead. He knew pain and sadness were painted on his face. There were still those he mourned. Horrible, unnecessary deaths that would never disappear from his mind completely. But perhaps that was a good thing. It reminded him of what was important in life and how fast it could all be gone.

"I'm sorry, Leith. I shouldn't have brought that up." There was regret in her eyes when he turned back to her.

"Do not worry, my angel." He let his gaze take in her beauty and concern for him. "A long life will have moments of pain. It is inevitable. And that is the only thing I will regret when we mate. I cannot prevent pain from touching your life at some point."

She chuckled, but there was no humor in her eyes. "You forget that there are moments of pain in every life no matter how short."

He smiled at her, but he could feel that it was somewhat forced. "You are right, of course. I guess I am not as attuned to humans and their struggles anymore. Perhaps I have kept myself separate for too long. I do not watch television, and I rarely speak with humans. Most of what goes on in the world does not concern me, and I try not to think about it because there is not much I can do to improve it without exposing myself and others like me." Turning away, he almost winced at his own words. They made him seem oblivious and uncaring. Not exactly traits he wanted to advertise to his future mate, but at least he had spoken the truth.

A tugging on his hand made him stop and turn to face Sabrina.

She was staring up at him with an expression of concern on her face. "You've seen too many people die haven't you?"

It wasn't what he had expected her to say. "Of course. I am three hundred years old, Sabrina. Several generations of people have died in my lifetime."

"No." She shook her head. "What I mean is, you've seen too many people you've cared about die. And that's the real reason you've stopped spending time with humans. It's too painful when they go."

Images of broken bodies forced their way to the front of his mind before he could prevent it, tearing a sound of pain from him. So many good people gone.

Arms wrapped around his neck and pulled him into a tight hug. She didn't say anything, just held him close. He couldn't remember anyone ever doing that to him before, but it felt good. The pain that had gripped him slowly released its hold, and he wrapped his arms around her and buried his face in the crook of her neck. Sabrina was much too young to have experienced what he was talking about, yet she understood perfectly.

Slowly, he loosened his hold on her and lifted his head to stare into her beautiful blue eyes. "Thank you, my angel."

"Anytime." She smiled up at him, before her eyes dropped to his lips.

"Not interrupting anything, am I?"

The voice came from behind Leith, but he immediately knew whom it belonged to. "Yes, you are, Aidan." Sabrina dropped her arms from around his neck, and Leith turned toward the other man.

"Nice to see you again, Leith. It's been a long time." Aidan grinned at him as they shook hands before turning his attention to Sabrina. "And this lovely lady is?"

Sabrina extended her hand, but as soon as she came into contact with Aidan's fingers, she pulled hers back with a hiss like she had somehow burned herself.

Leith felt himself frowning. He had no idea what had just happened. Aidan was a special type of supernatural with extraordinary powers, but he would never hurt anyone.

"That's new." Cocking his head, Aidan studied Sabrina's face like she was something he had never encountered before. And that was astonishing, because if there was anyone who knew the variety of supernaturals that existed in the world, it would be Aidan.

Leith put his arm around Sabrina's waist and pulled her close. "What happened, my angel?"

She didn't meet his gaze but kept staring at Aidan with her eyes narrowed like she didn't trust him.

"What did you feel when you touched me?" Aidan kept staring at Sabrina like she was an interesting puzzle he would like to solve. "You reacted like you burned yourself or suffered an electric shock, but I didn't feel anything."

Instead of answering Aidan's question, Sabrina put her arms around Leith's waist and held him tight. She tipped her head back and met Leith's gaze. "How well do you know this man?"

Leith felt his jaw slacken in astonishment as he stared into her fierce gaze. She wasn't asking because she was scared but because she wanted to protect him. *Him*. A powerful shifter. A warm feeling spread through his chest as he stared into her intense blue eyes. His mate was magnificent. Powerful and protective. And so damn sexy.

"I take it this is your future mate." Aidan chuckled. "It shouldn't come as a surprise that someone like you would find someone unique."

Leith found himself frowning as he swung his gaze to Aidan. "What do you mean?"

"No, no, no." Aidan grinned at him. "If you don't know yet, I'm not going to spoil the surprise. You'll find out soon enough." He swung his gaze to Sabrina. "Good day to you, ma'am. It's been an honor."

Leith could only stare as Aidan walked away from them. He had no idea what the man had meant by Sabrina being unique. Of course she was unique in that she was his mate, but that wasn't what Aidan had been talking about.

"Who was that?" He could hear the suspicion in Sabrina's voice.

Looking down into her eyes, he smiled. *Unique.* She was definitely that to him, but Aidan had sensed something about her that made her special, and Leith had a feeling it was something more than the fact that she was a witch. "I cannot tell you who he is until we are mated, my angel. Hardly any supernaturals know who he is, and I have been sworn to secrecy. But there are no secrets between mates. That is an accepted fact."

"I've never met anyone like him before. His power is substantial and different." There was uncertainty in her gaze. Perhaps even fear. "He can cause a lot of destruction if he chooses."

Leith tightened his hold on her. "You are correct in that he is extremely powerful, but he uses those powers for good. You can trust me on that. I have known him for a long time and even helped him on a couple of occasions."

Sabrina took a deep breath while studying his face.

She didn't look convinced in the least. "Okay, I hear what you're saying, but I reserve the right to be skeptical until I know more about him."

He burst out laughing. Many shifters and even other supernaturals came to him for advice. They might question his comments at times, but they revered his opinions and trusted his words. He knew he was considered an authority on anything supernatural, and a valued discussion partner in other matters as well. Except with his mate. She didn't take his word for anything, apparently, choosing to decide for herself.

CHAPTER 8

"Thank you for dinner, Leith. I can understand why you like that restaurant." Sabrina could feel his subdued power radiating from behind her as she walked in front of him up the stairs to their suite. Their suite. She hadn't really considered the implications of that until this moment. There was only one bed, and even though it was large, it wasn't nearly large enough to prevent her body from heating from his proximity.

"I am glad you like it, my angel. It is my favorite." His voice caressed her body as it flowed over her, and a small shiver raced down her spine. It was like her body was becoming more aware of him with every passing hour, and that wasn't a good thing.

They arrived at the door to their suite, and Leith unlocked it before allowing her to enter ahead of him. Her eyes landed on the large couch. She had cleared away her things earlier, so there was room to sit, and as she planned, to lie down. Sleeping next to Leith wasn't an option.

The door closed behind them, and she turned to him. He was by far the most attractive man she had ever met, with his dark-green eyes and typically somber expression. But when he smiled, he was nothing less than gorgeous. His long copper-colored hair was in a ponytail at the moment, but it did nothing to detract from his masculinity.

His laughter, though, had taken her completely by surprise. Until hearing that sound, she had thought his most dangerous feature was his wicked smile. But that had changed when he laughed. The sound had hit all her nerve endings like he was touching her in her most intimate places. It had made her squirm as heat coiled in her belly, and she had quickly turned her head away and pulled her shoulders up, like she was cold, to hide his laughter's effect on her.

Sabrina had wanted to hear his laughter since she'd first met him, but after experiencing its effect on her, she realized she needed to avoid that sound. If she was going to be able to keep control of her powers and sanity, she had to make sure not to make him laugh.

"When are we going to visit the panther clan tomorrow?" She smiled up at him, focusing on acting as normal and unaffected by him as possible.

"Nine, so I suggest we get some sleep." One corner of his mouth curved slightly, and a smidgen of heat lightened his eyes.

Desire raced through her, and she quickly tore her gaze away from his. "Okay, I'll take the couch." Quickly walking away from him, she headed toward her bag in the corner. She needed to put distance between them. Just knowing he was within touching distance was enough to test her self-control.

"Sabrina, we can sleep in the same bed without—"

"No! We can't." She turned toward him and met his gaze across the room.

He frowned. "I will never do anything you do not want me to do, my angel. You want to maintain control when there are other people close by. I understand and respect that."

Closing her eyes, she swallowed hard. She didn't doubt his words. He was an honorable and caring man. But he didn't know the extent of her powers, and he probably wouldn't stop her if she touched him. And if she lost control, he would be the first one to be hurt.

Opening her eyes, she noticed he had cut the distance between them in half. "Leith, stop. Please."

His eyes narrowed, and there was a mixture of hurt and anger in them, but he did as she asked. "I just want to be close to you. You can trust me."

She bit her bottom lip hard while contemplating what to say to him. But there was really just one option, to be honest with him. "I know, and I trust you. But I don't trust myself around you."

Widening in surprise, his eyes rapidly changed from dark green to bright emerald. His jaw tensed, and he took a step toward her before he seemed to realize what he was doing and stopped. "You want me just as much as I want you."

It wasn't a question, but Sabrina nodded anyway.

"We should leave." Licking his lips slowly, his eyes dipped to her breasts before moving farther down. "Go somewhere remote where we can be completely alone."

A shiver racked her body before she fisted her

hands at her side in an effort to maintain control. "No, Leith. We're going to stay here and do our best to find Ambrosia."

His eyes snapped back up to hers. "The mating bond is pulling us together, my angel, and I am not the only one feeling it. How long do you think we will be able to ignore it?"

Anger surged through her at the idea that their mating was somehow predestined or inevitable. It went against every fiber of her being to be forced into anything, even mating this amazing man. Control was her religion. She had lived by it for more than ten years, and she wasn't going to stop now. If she at some stage chose to mate him because she felt it was safe to do so, that was okay, but she wouldn't allow herself to be forced into it before she was ready.

"I will ignore it for however long I feel it's necessary." Sabrina grabbed her bag of toiletries and stormed past him into the bathroom.

After closing the door behind her, she just stood there. She had just acted like a stubborn two-year-old. How mature was that? But this need inside her to go to him and give in to her desire was starting to scare her, and even though Leith was a fantastic man and would never intentionally hurt a fly if not strictly necessary, he didn't know what was at stake. She was the only one who did, and therefore, it was up to her to maintain control.

Taking a deep breath, she pushed all her feelings to the back of her mind. She could do this. It was only a matter of focusing on what was important. And at the moment, that was Ambrosia and preventing the evil witch from doing any more harm. They had to find out where she was and what she intended to do next, and perhaps more importantly why she wanted to increase her power.

Sabrina had never met the woman, but she had the feeling Ambrosia's main motivation was revenge. Maybe even revenge due to loss. It was based on a feeling Sabrina had gotten when she used her power to locate Julianne after she disappeared from Leith's house. And if that were the case, it would be hard to persuade Ambrosia to stop. Loss was always a powerful motivator, and not a lot could negate it.

There was a knock on the door, and Leith's voice sounded from the other side. "Sabrina, are you all right?"

She stared at the door for a couple of seconds. What she wouldn't give to be able to throw herself into Leith's arms and forget everything else. "Yes, I'm fine. I'll be out soon." Her voice sounded a bit odd to her own ears, but perhaps it wasn't as noticeable through the door.

"Okay, my angel. Take the time you need."

Right, get a grip. She dug through her toiletries for her toothbrush. They were going to visit both a panther clan and a wolfpack the next day, so she would be too busy to think about Leith and mating. That was a good thing. And hopefully the shifters they were going to talk to would have some useful information. Someone had to have met Ambrosia before and knew more about her.

After finishing in the bathroom, Sabrina stepped out of the room. Leith wasn't in the living room like she had expected, so she continued into the bedroom. Only to come to an abrupt stop right inside the door.

He was on the far side of the room with his back to her, unpacking his bag and putting his clothes away in the wardrobe. But that wasn't what had her staring. Corded muscles played just beneath his skin as he worked, clearly visible since he no longer had a shirt on. His jeans hung low on his hips, only held in place by his tight ass.

She must have made a sound because he suddenly turned around and stared at her. And that did nothing to impair her view. It wasn't the first time she had seen his bare chest, but for some reason, the impact was greater this time. Her fingers were itching to touch him, explore his defined abs, hard chest, and powerful shoulders and arms, and not necessarily in that order.

Her eyes dipped to his jeans or rather what she knew was hidden by his jeans. She had already felt his rather impressive package, and as she watched, he was quickly growing to that size again.

"Sabrina." The way he growled her name made her shudder, and a small moan escaped from her throat. "If you keep staring at me like that, I am not sure I will be able to keep my promise of not touching you. Your gaze is practically branding my skin it is so hot."

She dragged her gaze up to meet his and was shocked by the pent-up desire in his hooded emerald gaze. The sight made her channel clench and wetness soaked into her panties. "Leith." His name sounded more like a moan than a word, but apparently, he had no trouble understanding her. In less than a second, he had rounded the bed and closed the distance between them. Strong arms wrapped around her and pressed her against his solid chest a fraction of a second before his firm lips brushed against hers.

Need raked through her, and she threw her arms around his neck. Pulling him more firmly against her, she crushed her mouth to his just as he parted his lips and forced his tongue into her mouth. All thoughts left her mind, blown away by the taste and feel of him.

Their tongues dueled and caressed, stroked and plunged, reminding her of other activities. He was plundering her mouth like he wanted to devour her, but she was doing a pretty good job of plundering right back.

Standing on her toes with her breasts mashed against his hard chest, Sabrina wanted to feel his skin against her palms. Loosening her arms from around his neck, she let her fingers play along his neck and shoulders, marveling at the hard muscles playing underneath his smooth skin.

His arms disappeared from around her a second before her back hit the wall. Then his mouth left hers, and she couldn't help the whimper that escaped her at the loss of his hot mouth.

But he didn't leave her alone, only changed his attack on her senses. His hot lips traced a path along her jaw while his hands found their way beneath her shirt. His warm hands slowly caressed up her sides, and she held her breath in anticipation of what he would do next.

Sabrina moaned when he cupped her breasts through her bra, testing the weight of them in his hands. His thumbs caressed the bare skin along the top of her bra while he pushed his palms against her erect nipples, and she shivered as pleasure radiated from her sensitive peaks.

His mouth reached her ear, and his tongue gently

played along her earlobe. It didn't prepare her for what he did next. Teeth nipped her earlobe as his hot breath fanned the sensitive shell of her ear. At the same time, his fingers dipped into her bra and pinched her nipples. The double assault of pain and pleasure on her senses sent a shot of ecstasy directly to her clit, making her cry out his name as her pleasure button started throbbing with the need to be touched. More of her juices soaked into her panties, and she panted with the need to have Leith fill her.

Next thing she knew, strong hands gripped her hips and lifted her. She automatically wrapped her legs around his waist and gripped his powerful shoulders. He would never let her fall, she knew that, but something told her to hold on tight.

Leith stopped nibbling and licking her ear and pulled his head back to stare at her. His expression was pure seduction, with a wicked grin curving his sinful lips. Emerald heat blazed from his eyes, daring her to look away from him. This man knew exactly what he was doing to her. There was no hesitation or insecurity. He already knew where her buttons were and was just deciding in which order he wanted to push them. It was a good thing his strong arms were supporting her thighs, or she would have landed on her ass on the floor at his feet.

While holding her gaze captive, he pressed the thick ridge in his jeans firmly against her sensitive clit. A weird mewling noise left her throat when he started rubbing his hard length against her, and she felt her whole body tighten in preparation for release.

"No!" Sabrina would never know how she managed to break the thrall Leith had on her. It was nothing short of a miracle. "Leith, stop!" Her body was screaming for release, but that couldn't happen. She relaxed her legs, which were wrapped tightly around his waist.

The pressure against her clit eased when he pulled his lower body away from hers. Sadness showed in his eyes for a fraction of a second before he closed them and leaned forward to rest his forehead against hers. "I am sorry, my angel. I promised you that I would not…" He stopped like he didn't know what to say.

"No, this is my fault. You're just so… I didn't expect you to look so…" Heat suffused her face as she struggled to find words to describe him without choking. She had never told a man to his face that she found him attractive, and she was struggling to find appropriate words to describe him without sounding like an immature teenager. "Irresistible." A good word but not nearly sufficient to describe him and his effect on her.

He lifted his head and met her gaze. A smile tugged at his lips. "Irresistible. I like that you think so." He carefully set her down on her feet before cupping her cheeks. "You are everything to me, my angel. I have waited for you for centuries, but I had no idea that you were going to be so perfect. I cannot wait to make you mine, but I will try to be patient until you are ready, however long that may be."

Sabrina swallowed thickly as she stared into his emerald orbs. However long, indeed. What if she was never able to control her power? Chancing hurting him or even killing him wasn't something she was willing to do, so if she didn't find a way to control her power as she orgasmed, they would never be able to mate. And even if there was a way, she was quite sure that he wouldn't settle for a woman who could never give herself freely in bed.

"You seem so sure that everything will work out." She could feel herself frowning as she spoke. "That we'll be able to have sex like normal people."

He grinned. "Not like normal people. I want a lot more than normal people. But, yes, I am sure that everything will work out. You and I, we are meant to be together, my angel. And it will happen. Soon. I am confident of that."

Sabrina wasn't feeling confident at all, but there was no point mentioning that to Leith. He seemed to have made up his mind that this wasn't a big obstacle.

She sighed and put a small smile on her face. "We should get some sleep."

He let her go and straightened to his full height. It put all the muscles in his upper body on display, and she had to physically stop herself from letting her gaze travel down his mouthwatering body.

Taking a step to the side, she was about to head back into the living room when he stopped her. "You take the bed, and I will sleep on the couch. I will not have my mate sleeping on a simple sofa."

Sabrina smiled. "That's kind, but you're taller than me, so you'd probably be more comfortable in the bed."

"No." He crossed his arms over his chest, and she couldn't prevent herself from admiring the view this time. "I insist. You take the bed."

Struggling to remember what they were talking about, she forced her eyes back up to his. "Okay."

Leith ordered breakfast to be brought up to them in their suite. It was just over an hour until they were expected by the panther clan. Sabrina was in the shower, and he was restless and tired. A bit of a strange combination, but considering the pull of the mating bond and the fact that he had hardly had any sleep because of it, it was understandable.

Sabrina was scared. She was convinced she would hurt someone if she lost control of her powers. It had already happened at least once in her past. He remembered her words at the beach the previous morning. *I hurt someone, and that person will forever be altered because of my actions. The fact that I didn't mean it didn't change the outcome.*

He sighed and stared at the bathroom door. There had to be something he could do to convince her he was strong enough to handle it if she lost control. But so far all his attempts had failed, so he had to get her to agree to test her power on him. Perhaps actions would speak louder than words. They usually did.

There was a knock on the door, and he walked over and let the young man with their breakfast cart into the room. The food smelled delicious, but it wasn't enough to pull his thoughts away from his mate, not even for a second.

After the young man left, Sabrina stepped out of the bathroom. Turning to her, he tried to put a pleasant expression on his face, but it felt more like a grimace. He had always known that an unfulfilled mating bond was unpleasant, but experiencing how it strained his mind and body filled him with a newfound respect for those who managed to handle such a situation with grace and respect. At the moment all he wanted to do was pick up his mate, put her in the car, and find a remote place where they could mate without Sabrina worrying about other people's safety. His thoughts had been filled by her all night, and the few times he had actually fallen asleep, he had soon woken with his dick throbbing from a sexy dream of her.

"That smells delicious." Sabrina smiled at him as she moved over toward the table. "I didn't realize how hungry I am."

Leith hurried over to pull out the chair for her. "Good. Would you like some coffee?" The bar area was set up with a small coffee machine, and he moved over to it without waiting for her answer.

"Oh, yes." She sounded happy. "I need some caffeine to wake up properly."

He turned his head and studied her face as she smiled at him. She looked beautiful as always, but there were dark circles under her eyes. Maybe she had felt the pull of the mating bond all night as well. "Did you not sleep well, my angel?"

A slight blush rose in her cheeks. Breaking their eye contact, she pretended to find the food on her plate completely fascinating. "I slept okay."

It was an obvious lie, but he let it go. Pushing her to admit she was plagued by thoughts and dreams like he was, wasn't going to help her accept what was happening. In fact, it was more likely to drive her away. He already knew she was drawn to him, at least physically. She hadn't been able to conceal that the night before.

He put a cup of coffee in front of her before sitting

down to her left. His hunger was for other things than food at the moment, but he needed sustenance in order to maintain his self-control.

"How well do you know the panther alpha?" Sabrina's voice snapped him out of his thoughts, and he welcomed the change in topic.

He met her gaze. "Fairly well. Although I knew his father and grandfather better. They have succeeded each other as alpha for the clan, which is quite unusual. An alpha male is not guaranteed an alpha child, so succession for several generations is rare."

She nodded slowly, her brows pulling together like something was bothering her. Leith wanted to ask what she was thinking, but he stopped himself. He had already been pushing her quite hard to stay with him and accept him, but even though she was attracted to him, she hadn't responded well to being pushed. If she felt like he was backing her into a corner, at some point she might snap and leave. He didn't want to find out at which point that was.

"What happens to children born to a shifter and human mixed couple? Do they become shifters or human?" She frowned as she stared at him.

Relief released the tension in his shoulders, and he smiled. "Children of shifters are always shifters. At least I have never heard of any exceptions to that rule."

"And if two shifters of different kinds mate, like a panther and wolf, what then?"

Leith had a feeling where this was going. "That is determined when the child shifts for the first time. It can be wolf and panther."

Her frown became more pronounced. "You mean a

mix?"

Leith shook his head once. "No, forgive me for being imprecise. The child is either a wolf or a panther. Never a mix. But one kind is not favored over the other. The likelihood of the child being a wolf is the same as the likelihood of it being a panther."

Sabrina nodded. "Okay. So one shifter kind is not more dominant genetically than another. Is that what you are saying?"

Leith sighed. "For most shifter kinds, yes, but there are a few exceptions."

"And your kind is one of them." She held his gaze like she wanted to see his reaction to her statement.

This was what he had expected, but he wasn't sure how she felt about it. Her expression was carefully schooled and didn't give away what she was thinking. "Yes, my kind is dominant to every other kind. Except perhaps one."

"Perhaps?" Raising an eyebrow in question, she waited for his response.

"Yes, perhaps. I have never heard of a pairing of my kind with this rare kind of shifter, so I don't know whether one would be dominant to the other." Leith didn't elaborate. He had already given her more information than he should have before they were mated.

Taking a bite of his food, he waited to see what she was going to do with that information. But to his surprise, she didn't ask any more questions; instead, she focused on her food.

They finished their breakfast in silence. Leith wanted to say something to lighten the tone between them, but it was like someone had poured syrup into his mind. It was slow and sluggish, and he couldn't come up with anything remotely interesting to say.

Sabrina put down her knife and fork, and Leith looked at her. "Are you ready to go, my angel?"

"Yes." She rose and started gathering their plates, but Leith stopped her with a hand on her arm.

"Let the staff take care of this. They are happy to do it, and I am happy to pay them for it." He lifted his hand and traced a finger lightly down one smooth cheek. "You are very beautiful today."

Her eyes widened, and a rosy blush bloomed on her cheeks like before. "Thank you."

His eyes dipped to her mouth for a second. He wanted to feel her soft lips against his again, but this wasn't the time. They needed to leave or they'd be late.

CHAPTER 9

Sabrina studied the scenery while they drove east. According to Leith it was only about twenty minutes' drive from the hotel to the big house that served as the panther clan's headquarters. They didn't all live in the main house but were spread around in houses close by, forming their own little village. To anyone not knowing they were shifters, it looked just like any other village.

She wasn't quite sure what to expect from these people. It was the first time she visited a shifter group with an alpha leader. All the shifters she had met so far were individuals that didn't belong to a group or, as in Michael's case, were far away from the shifter group they belonged to. It would be interesting to see how the group dynamics worked and how they behaved toward each other.

Leith pulled up and parked in front of a large house. Within seconds three men and two women stepped out onto the porch like a welcoming party. It was obvious who the alpha was among them. His dominating posture and direct stare gave him away immediately, as well as the way the others held back and allowed him to take center stage.

Leith didn't turn to look at her as he spoke. "Please stay in your seat until I open the door for you." It was a request, but even though his tone was soft, it felt more like a command.

Sabrina chose not to wait, but stepped out onto the gravel just as Leith rounded the back end of the car.

"You should have waited." There was a frown on his face when he met her eyes. "Etiquette means something among shifters."

It was her turn to frown, and she cocked her head in question. But instead of explaining, he grabbed her hand and started walking toward the porch, obviously expecting her to follow him without objections.

It felt like a reprimand, and she didn't like it. Particularly because she was just realizing there were expectations with regard to her behavior, and she had no idea what those expectations were. It would have been nice if Leith had taken the time to explain the rules of shifter etiquette before they arrived. Until a minute ago, she had felt relatively comfortable about this visit, but she didn't anymore. How could she when she had no idea if what she did or said could be misunderstood or even taken as an insult? She was also ticked off at Leith for not telling her what she needed to know to act correctly.

Sabrina used the opportunity to study the alpha as they approached the house. He was a handsome man with dark, cropped hair—military style. His posture and clothing screamed military as well, with his all-black cargo pants, tank top, and combat boots. He was tall, but more noticeable was his width. Thick shoulders and arms like tree trunks were on display, and his chest and abs were giving his tank top a run for its money. His lower body adhered to the same muscular template.

Those characteristics were enough to make sure he caught the attention of women and men alike wherever he went, but none of them were his most prominent feature. Elaborate tattoos covered most of his skin. Intricate designs curled around his arms and shoulders and spread to his chest and even his head. The only part she could see that wasn't covered by tattoos was his face, unless he had some hidden beneath his thick black beard.

"Leith. Nice to see you again." The alpha moved forward as soon as they stepped onto the porch, and Leith and the alpha gripped each other's forearms the way she had seen Leith and Duncan greet each other two days before. It confirmed what she had thought: that it was a typical greeting between shifters.

"Bryson. You too." Leith let go of the other man's forearm before turning to look at Sabrina. "This is Sabrina."

"A pleasure to meet you, Sabrina." Bryson's dark-brown eyes met hers, before he gave her a small bow. Apparently she didn't qualify for the gripping of forearms, but that was expected. None of the other shifters she had met had greeted a woman that way, but then she had never met a female shifter before. It was another question to ask Leith later.

"It's a pleasure to meet you, too, Bryson." She gave him a small nod.

Leith seemed to stiffen beside her at the same time as Bryson's lips stretched into a cocky grin. Then the alpha turned on his heel and headed back into the house. Leith tightened his grip on her hand and started after the alpha, and she fell into step beside him.

She had just said or done something wrong. Leith's body language and Bryson's facial expression had both confirmed it, but she had absolutely no idea what she had done that was inappropriate or carried a different meaning than she had intended. As far as she could understand, she had just been polite.

The alpha's entourage followed them into the house, and she could hear them murmuring between them. Someone even chuckled, and she didn't like the sound of it. It had something to do with her behavior or words.

They were led into a large living room with sofas and chairs forming several seating groups around the room. Bryson continued to the far corner of the room, where he took a seat in a large armchair placed strategically for him to be able to see the whole room and the door, before indicating for them to sit on the sofa to his left. Three of his people sat down on the sofa facing them across the coffee table, which left one young woman standing next to Bryson.

The alpha looked at Leith before moving his gaze to Sabrina. "Euna will take your orders for hot drinks. What would you like?" Bryson indicated the woman standing beside him but kept his gaze on Sabrina while he spoke.

"Coffee for us both, please, Bryson." Leith's voice was measured and polite, but a hint of power flowed into Sabrina through the hand he was still holding firmly in his. His power slid through her, making her aware of how little space there was between their bodies.

Smirking, the alpha nodded before turning to Euna. "Coffee for the table, please, Euna." The young woman immediately turned and hurried out of the room.

Sabrina felt herself frowning as she studied Leith's profile. He didn't turn to meet her gaze, and the fact that he didn't irritated her. Leith hadn't made decisions for her like this before. He was correct that she would like coffee, but to not give her a choice felt disrespectful and highhanded. He wasn't her boss or her superior, and even if he had been, he still should have given her a choice.

Swinging her gaze back to Bryson, she put a smile on her face. "Would it be okay to ask for a cup of tea instead of coffee?"

Leith's head snapped around, and she could feel his eyes on her, but she didn't meet his gaze. He hadn't acknowledged her before, so why should she pay him any attention now?

Surprise showed on the alpha's face for a second before he grinned. "Of course, Sabrina. No trouble at all." He waved his hand at the man sitting closest to him, and the man immediately rose and left the room. Probably to tell Euna of Sabrina's preference for tea.

Leith's power amped up and started flowing into her through her hand at a level that was making her uncomfortable in the presence of these people. A simmering heat was settling low in her belly, and it was making her squirm. She met Leith's gaze and was shocked to see the anger there, but when she tried to pull her hand out of his hold, he tightened his grip.

"Please excuse us." Leith suddenly rose and sent a burst of power into her that made her shoot up from her seat. "We will be right back."

Without waiting for a response from Bryson, Leith pulled her none too gently out of the room and out of the house. He didn't stop until they were next to the car, then without warning, he pushed her front against the side of the car before pressing his body flush against her back, effectively locking her in place.

"You are mine, Sabrina." Leith's mouth was right next to her ear, and his breath fanned hot across the sensitive skin of her neck and ear when he spoke. His voice was low and filled with anger and power, and it was making her squirm and pant with need.

"Leith." She wanted to object to his possessive behavior, but all she managed to do was moan his name. How she could be so turned on was disturbing, but she couldn't help it. His power felt like liquid fire flowing into her veins and touching her everywhere.

"Bryson wants you, Sabrina. He is not mated, and he has a thing for beautiful blond women. And if he can lure you from someone powerful like me, all the better. He is a man of integrity otherwise, but he has a thing for stealing other men's women. Unless they are mated. But since we are not, I could not present you as my mate, and he now considers you fair game.

"By showing him that you accede to my authority, he will back off. Otherwise, he will flirt with you and try to take you from me. It won't happen, of course, because I will fight him for you if I have to, but I would rather that it did not come to that. I will win without a problem since I am far more powerful than he is, but it will put a dent in his pride and will make it hard to maintain a civil tone between us in the future. I will forever be his rival."

Leith sighed and eased off her back. When he spoke again, the anger was gone from his voice. "I am sorry, my angel. I should have told you what to expect before we got here. I just never expected Bryson to try anything with my woman, but as soon as I saw the expression on his face, when he stepped out of the house and caught sight of you in the car, I realized that I had made a mistake."

Sabrina took a deep breath and tried to force her body to calm down. "Please let me go, Leith. I don't fall for arrogant assholes, and I really don't want to put you in that category."

Leith stepped back and let her turn around. The anger was gone from his eyes, replaced by something that looked like regret.

She wanted to be angry with him for not trusting her to say no to someone like Bryson. The alpha panther was a handsome man, and probably charming if he wanted to be, but he was too arrogant and smooth to ever tempt her. And she had no problem saying no to men she didn't like. Even men she did like she had turned down with relative ease in the past.

"I want to be angry with you for not trusting me." She stared into Leith's eyes, and his jaw tensed at her words. "But I understand that you acted the way you did to protect me. For future reference, though, please remember that I'm not a weak and stupid woman who doesn't know how to take care of herself."

Leith flinched but kept his gaze locked with hers. "I am sorry, Sabrina. It has never once crossed my mind that you are weak and stupid. Stubborn on the other hand..." He let the sentence hang, his expression unreadable.

Sabrina knew they were being watched. Bryson was following their exchange from one of the windows in the house. She could practically feel his gaze on them. Leith wanted to make sure the alpha knew whom she belonged to, and even though she didn't yet belong to Leith and perhaps never would, she did agree with him that Bryson needed to get the message that she wasn't interested or available for his amusement.

She closed the distance to the tall, gorgeous, and somewhat maddening man in front of her and threw her arms around his neck. His eyes widened in surprise when she rose to her toes and put her mouth on his. But his surprise didn't last long. With a groan, he wrapped his arms around her and kissed her back with an intensity that took her breath away. His tongue stroked into her mouth and caressed hers in a way that heated her body from within. And she responded in kind, rubbing her tongue against his while she pressed her breasts against his hard chest.

When they finally broke apart, she was breathing hard. She might have started the kiss, but he had quickly taken over and shown her who was in charge. And she'd enjoyed it. Which was strange since she generally liked to be in control. But when he took over, she melted like ice cream in the sun. It felt so good to be at his mercy, and yet it was exactly what she couldn't allow to happen. Control was everything.

His eyes glowed bright emerald as he stared down at her. "Anytime you want to do that again, just tell me. Or better yet, show me the way you just did." A wicked grin split his face, and Sabrina's jaw slackened as she stared up at him. That grin was devastating to her control, robbing her mind of her will to stay away from him.

"I think Bryson will leave you alone now, my angel." His eyes were slowly dimming to their normal dark green, but the panty-dropping grin was still in place. "Shall we go back inside?"

All she could do was nod. Her jaw didn't seem to be working properly, and her whole body was tingly and twitchy. If she had been able to think of a good excuse for them to leave immediately, she would have happily grabbed onto it with both hands. But they were visiting these people for a reason, and they had to complete what they had set out to do.

Bryson didn't look at her when they entered the living room. There was a smirk on his face, but it seemed forced as he gave a small nod of acknowledgement to Leith. Apparently, she wasn't worthy of his attention any more now that he knew she wasn't interested in his advances. And that was completely okay with her.

They sat down on the sofa they had vacated a few minutes before. Their hot drinks had arrived, and Sabrina busied herself with adding sweetener and milk to her tea while Leith started recounting what they had learned of Ambrosia so far.

Bryson narrowed his eyes. "Sounds like she can strike anywhere at any time with any shifter. Doesn't really narrow down our search now, does it? You have no clue as to who this woman really is or her motivation?"

Leith shook his head once. "Unfortunately, no. We

have friends who can recognize her on sight, but we have had no luck finding her real identity. The car she used when she picked up Julianne not far from my house was Steven's, and questioning him did not tell us anything we did not already know. She never disclosed any personal information to him."

Nodding slowly, Bryson seemed to consider the information Leith had given him. "Witches. I had no idea they could be powerful enough to ever threaten or manipulate a shifter."

Sabrina's head snapped up, and she stared at the alpha sitting in the large armchair at the end of the table. He had already known about witches before he had been informed about Ambrosia. And from what she had heard from the shifters she had gotten to know in the last few days, that was unusual. "When did you first hear about witches?"

Bryson swung his gaze to her for a second before moving it back to Leith. "A couple of years ago, but they are nothing like the woman you're talking about. Just a mother and her adult daughter using their weak power to grow herbs and flowers in their garden. Not exactly a threat to anyone, although the daughter is a stunner." A grin spread across the alpha's face. "Playing hard to get, but I have time. She'll give in soon enough. I can see she wants me too." The grin turned a bit strained as his gaze passed over Sabrina, before landing on his cup of coffee that suddenly seemed to be fascinating.

Sabrina wanted to ask him more questions about these women. It would have been great to get to know other witches, and after finding out about shifters and the fact that they all seemed to know about each other, she couldn't help thinking that if witches had a similar network, it would have been much easier to locate Ambrosia. Because the evil witch had to have come from somewhere and witch power usually ran in families.

"There is an angle we have not worked yet." Leith kept his gaze on Bryson. "And it might be something you can help with."

The alpha's gaze lifted to meet Leith's. "Go on."

"We have not questioned Jack Williams yet. Do you know him?"

From the look of disgust on Bryson's face, there was no doubt that he did, and clearly there was no love lost between the two panthers. "As well as I ever want to. He's an asshole and a criminal. But you want me to talk to him."

It wasn't a question, but Leith answered him anyway. "Yes. You may not like him, but as a fellow panther you might be in a better position to get him talking than anyone else. Stephanie, the woman he planned to mate against her will, has told us everything she knows about Ambrosia. But Jack might know more about the evil witch. As far as we have been able to find out, he is still not fully healed after being burned alive, but that might be to your advantage."

Bryson nodded slowly. "Perhaps. I'll have to consider how to approach him to be able to extract as much information as I can about Ambrosia."

Euna entered the room and walked up to stand beside the alpha's chair before turning to address the people around the table. "Would anyone like some more coffee?" Her eyes landed on Sabrina, not quite meeting her gaze. "Or tea?"

Sabrina shook her head while giving the young woman a small smile. Euna seemed anxious around people like someone had hurt her. But Sabrina didn't get the impression that the someone was in this room. If anything the woman seemed to feel safe around Bryson, like he was her savior and protector.

Several people including Leith wanted more coffee, and Sabrina expected the young woman to leave when she had her answers, but instead she kept standing beside Bryson with an uncertain expression on her face.

"Speak, Euna. You know you don't need my permission to say what's on your mind." There was a tenderness in Bryson's gaze when he looked up at Euna, like a big brother for a baby sister, but their vastly different appearances suggested they weren't closely related.

Sabrina felt her respect for the alpha grow significantly. Leith had been right. This man might be a womanizer, but he had some redeeming qualities. Euna had clearly been through something bad, but Bryson was trying to rebuild her confidence and sense of self-worth.

"I thought…" Euna stopped, and her gaze lowered to her feet.

"Go on, Euna." Bryson put his hand lightly on the young woman's upper arm and gave her an encouraging smile. "What is it you would like to tell us? I have a feeling it's important."

Euna raised her head and met Sabrina's gaze. "I know this Ambrosia." The young woman's eyes widened like she was a bit shocked to hear her own words. "I mean… I don't know her, but I've heard the name before. And it's an unusual name, so maybe it's the same woman. Because you're talking about a woman?"

Sabrina nodded and smiled, trying to project as much encouragement as she could with her smile. "Yes, Ambrosia is a woman. Where did you hear her name?"

"From my sister." Pain flitted across the young woman's face. "My wolf sister. A woman in my... I mean, a woman in her pack died, and the woman's mother was called Ambrosia."

Bryson's expression hardened with anger, but his hand remained lightly touching Euna's arm. "Are you talking about the human woman who was mated to the second alpha?"

Euna nodded with a poorly concealed wince. "Yes, her. Her mother's name was Ambrosia."

"Thank you, Euna." Bryson squeezed her arm lightly. "This is valuable information."

A small happy smile curved Euna's lips before she abruptly turned away. "I'll get your coffee now." Then she hurried out of the room.

CHAPTER 10

Leith nodded at the door Euna had just disappeared through while keeping his eyes on Bryson. "Do you know more about this second alpha and his human mate?"

Bryson pulled in a deep breath before his gaze settled on Leith. "Euna was raised in the wolfpack located just to the north of Inverness. Until a year ago, it was ruled by a bastard who considered women property to be owned and dominated. Well not just women, actually. Some of the weaker men were treated the same way too. A year ago, Henry, a young and powerful alpha from the pack far north, swooped in and killed the old alpha before anyone knew what was happening. He had watched the pack for some time and knew how they were suffering under the old alpha's rule. So as soon as Henry was powerful enough, he struck.

"Most people accepted the change of leadership without complaint. I think they were relieved and happy to have a leader who cared about them. But a few of the old alpha's most-trusted men didn't, and they wanted to continue the old traditions of the pack. Among them was a second, weaker alpha who had his eyes set on Euna. Henry found out in time to prevent the forced mating, and he asked me if Euna could stay with us for a time. That was more than six months ago. The second alpha wasn't happy with that, of course, and came here claiming she was his true mate. He got a sound beating and was sent on his way, but considering what happened next, I regret not killing him when I had the chance. He picked up a human girl and mated her against her will."

Leith nodded. "Yes, we heard about the forced mating. He killed her a few weeks later."

"Well." Bryson frowned. "The jury's still out on that one. Some say he killed her, and some say she killed herself. Nobody really knows. They had left the pack by then and were living somewhere out west. However, according to Euna, his mate's mother was called Ambrosia. And if she's the same Ambrosia you're looking for, then I'd say her motivation for doing whatever she's doing is revenge."

"I agree." Leith nodded again. "And I have a feeling this is the same Ambrosia we are looking for. We are going to meet with Henry and his pack later today, but based on this new information, I think we need to talk to the second alpha as well if he is still around. Do you have any idea where he might be located, or do you think Euna does?"

Bryson shook his head slowly. "I don't know where he's at, but we can ask Euna if she has any ideas where to look for him. He hasn't shown up here after we beat him up, but we've kept an eye out. I wouldn't put it past that asshole to show up again to try to take Euna, but if he does, he'll be begging for death by the time we're finished with him. There's no mercy for scum like him."

"I fully agree." Leith still found it hard to believe that a shifter would kill his own mate. Even if she wasn't his true mate, the bond between mates was strong and losing her would be devastating mentally as well as physically. It made more sense if the woman had chosen to end her own life. If she was forced to mate with the wolf, being bonded to a person she didn't want, perhaps even hated, could certainly have pushed her to choose death over staying with him.

Euna entered the room with a pot of coffee and quickly refilled their cups. Just as she was about to head out of the room, Bryson addressed the young woman.

"Thank you, Euna. Before you go, I'd like to ask you another question."

"Okay." The young woman nodded and went to stand next to the alpha's chair.

Bryson smiled up at Euna and put a hand on her upper arm like he wanted to reassure her. "Don't be alarmed, Euna. Remember that you're safe here with us. We're trying to locate the asshole. Do you have any idea where he might be staying? Any suggestions you have are helpful."

Leith studied the young woman. It was obvious the asshole was their chosen nickname for the alpha who had intended to claim Euna as his mate. And seeing her flinch again at the mention of him, there might be a good reason they called him that instead of using his given name.

"I…" Euna stumbled and visibly swallowed before she continued. "I'm not sure, but he sometimes went to visit a woman up near Tain. That's the only place I can think of. He didn't leave the pack grounds often."

"Do you happen to know the woman's name or her address?" Bryson smiled encouragingly at the young woman, but she only shook her head in response to his question.

"That's okay, Euna." Bryson squeezed her arm lightly before removing his hand. "What you've been able to tell us is valuable. Thank you."

Without looking at anyone else around the table, the young woman hurried out of the room.

Bryson turned to meet Leith's gaze. "If she remembers anything else useful, I'll tell you, but I'm not going to make her answer any more questions about him. I've encouraged her to forget he exists, because dwelling on the past prevents her from moving forward. But if she says something, I'll get in touch."

"Sounds good." Leith nodded. "We will be talking to Henry this afternoon. He might know something. At least now we have an idea who Ambrosia is. That is more than we had when we came. Thank you for your help, Bryson."

"My pleasure." The panther alpha rose to indicate that their visit was over.

Leith took Sabrina's hand in his before he stood, and she got up when he did.

"Keep in touch, Leith." Bryson's gaze strayed to Sabrina for half a second before swinging back to Leith. "And please tell us if there's anything more we can do. Ambrosia is a threat to all of us, and we're happy to help any way we can."

"Thank you, Bryson." Leith gave him a short nod in acknowledgement of his offer. "Just keep your eyes and ears open for any relevant information."

"Will do." Bryson gave him a nod back.

Tightening his grip on Sabrina's hand, Leith made his way out of the house. Bryson was showing his respect and acknowledging Leith's superior power by not escorting them out of his house. It was a show of deference, according to the old customs, and in Bryson's case most likely a form of apology for showing an interest in Sabrina.

Leith escorted Sabrina to the car and opened the door for her. He waited for her to take a seat before closing the door. She didn't object to his taking control this time, but even if she had, Bryson had gotten the message, and Leith didn't expect any more unwanted attention from the panther.

As soon as they were out on the road, he glanced at Sabrina. She was staring straight ahead with an unreadable expression on her face, and he couldn't help wondering whether she was still angry with him for his behavior earlier. Though her kiss had convinced him of her acceptance of his apology at the time, he was starting to wonder whether that had been a bit premature. This was all new to her, and she hadn't met any shifters who put much emphasize on the old customs until Bryson.

"Do we have time to stop by Culloden Moor before we go back to the hotel?" Sabrina turned to look at him, but he was too shocked by her question to meet her gaze. "I've never been there, and it's such a significant place in Scottish history."

Leith had to concentrate not to shudder at the thought of that place. If he never saw it again in his life, it would be too soon, but he couldn't say no to Sabrina. If she wanted to see the place of the final destructive battle between the Jacobites and the British army, he would take her there. "We can stop there for a little while, I suppose." His voice sounded normal, even though his mind was telling him visiting the place of the bloody battle wasn't a good idea.

They pulled into the big parking lot outside the visitor center and were lucky to find a vacant spot among all the tourists who had decided to visit the place that day. Leith wouldn't have complained if the place had been so packed that they couldn't find anywhere to park, but unfortunately he wasn't that lucky.

Leith took Sabrina's hand in his and met her gaze as they walked toward the battlefield. She smiled at him, but he wasn't able to smile back. Just the thought of where they were was causing his heart to speed up and sweat to form on his forehead and his back, but he was determined to hold it together for her.

The grass was cut in large sections of the field, but apart from that it wasn't much different from what he remembered. Well, except for the stones raised in memory of the battle and the people who died there. He had never laid eyes on those before.

"It feels incredible walking around a place where history was made." Sabrina's eyes wandered around the area, taking in the field with awe in her gaze. "I've read about the battle and this place and seen plenty of pictures, but being here is a completely different and more powerful experience than I ever imagined. Can you feel it?"

Oh, he could feel it all right, and it was powerful, but it wasn't the same feeling Sabrina had. Not even in the same ballpark. She probably thought she had some idea of what had happened on Culloden Moor, like so many others did when they visited this place or others like it, but he knew for a fact she didn't. Only people who had been to war and survived knew what it was like. Anyone else just thought they did.

"Leith?" Sabrina's questioning voice pulled him out of his thoughts. "Are you all right? You look pale, and you're breathing and sweating like you've been running flat out for miles."

He met her worried gaze. She was standing directly in front of him with her hands on his chest, and he hadn't even noticed they had stopped. His breathing was labored, and his stomach was rolling and twisting, threatening to make him throw up. Taking a deep breath, he tried to gain control of his physical reaction to the place. "I will go back to the car. You go ahead and see what you want to see."

He turned to leave, but instead of letting him go, Sabrina grabbed his hand and walked back toward the car with him. She didn't say anything, just walked quietly beside him until they reached the car.

"I am sorry, Sabrina." Leith turned to face her and met her eyes. Her expression was still one of concern. "I thought I would be able to handle it, but apparently I was wrong."

"You were here in 1746." It wasn't a question. Staring up at him with a frown, she shook her head slowly. "You should've told me that you didn't want to see this place again. I would never have asked to go if I'd known."

Leith sighed, staring at the beautiful woman in front of him. "I am not very good at communicating, am I? I should have told you what to expect and how to behave before we went to talk to the panthers, but I did not. I should have told you that I have no wish to ever see this place again, but I did not. And instead of telling you about being my mate in a calm and open manner, I declared that you are mine like you are property to be owned. I am sorry, Sabrina. It seems I have been on my own too long and no longer know how to care for someone else. Perhaps I never did."

Sabrina closed the distance between them and put her arms around his neck. Her expression was still one of concern when she spoke. "Don't be so hard on yourself. Communication is a skill that nobody will ever be able to master to perfection because people are not perfect. What is clear to one person is completely unintelligible to another, and adding time into the mix only makes it worse. Let's go back to the hotel and relax for a little while. We still have a few hours until we're going to visit the pack."

Leith nodded as he stared into his mate's beautiful blue eyes filled with concern and compassion for him. After Culloden, he had avoided relationships with women that might develop into something more. Just the thought of losing someone he had come to care about due to sickness or old age was enough to make him keep everyone at an arm's length, at least emotionally. He'd had lovers from time to time, but he had made sure that no deeper feelings were involved. But with Sabrina there was no need to hold back; at least it wouldn't be when he could finally persuade her to mate him.

After getting back into the car, they drove to the hotel in silence. But it wasn't an uncomfortable silence. Sabrina's hand was on his thigh, and he could feel her acceptance and support, even though she didn't say anything.

As soon as they parked, Sabrina was out the door, and she quickly rounded the car to meet him when he stepped out. There was a light in her eyes and an eagerness in her movements that he wasn't able to interpret.

Smiling, she grabbed his hand. "Come. I have something to show you."

"Show me?" Leith let himself get tugged along toward the private entrance to their suite. "What are you going to show me?"

"Not yet. I said show you, not tell you." There was a grin on her face, but she didn't look at him as they entered the hotel and started up the stairs.

She was up to something, and he found himself curious as to what it was. From what he had learned about Sabrina so far, she wasn't the impulsive type, but she wasn't averse to adventure either, as long as she could stay in control of her emotions.

As soon as he had closed the door to the suite behind them, Sabrina's arms wrapped around his neck. Her lips were on his, but he was so stunned by her sudden kiss it took him a couple of seconds to respond.

When his mind finally caught up with what was happening, he wrapped his arms around her and moved his lips against her soft ones. She parted her lips, and her tongue licked the seam of his mouth, and he didn't let the invitation go unanswered. He opened his mouth and licked the tip of her tongue before sliding his tongue against hers. The taste and feel of her was amazing, and his body required no more encouragement to wake up and anticipate more.

"Sabrina," he murmured against her lips. "My sweet angel." Her breasts were trapped against his chest, and his hands were itching to touch them and play with them. His mind was quickly narrowing down to one focus, effectively aided by the need to claim his mate.

Sabrina suddenly broke their kiss, and Leith opened his eyes to stare down at her. No doubt his eyes were shining emerald with his arousal, a clear indication of what he wanted. But she already knew that from feeling his hard cock against her belly. There was no hiding his attraction to her, but then why would he want to? She wouldn't have kissed him like that if she didn't want him to react.

There was a smile on her face when her arms disappeared from around his neck, and she took a step back. His front immediately felt desolate, and he was about to close the distance between them again when he felt her hand on his erection through the material of his jeans.

"Sabrina." Her name came out on a groan as his shaft hardened even more under her palm.

"I have something to show you, remember?" She flicked open the button of his jeans, before slowly pulling down the zipper.

His eyes were drawn to her hands. "I have seen that before."

Laughter burst from her, but it ended on a gasp

when his swollen member sprang free from his pants.

His gaze snapped to her face, taking in her wide eyes and half-open mouth as she stared at his cock. At least she didn't look disappointed. Not that he had expected her to.

Her hand closed around him, and he shuddered with pleasure. Her hand felt so soft when she moved it slowly up and down his length, and knowing that it was his angel touching him amped up the sensation tenfold.

"Come here." Her gaze rose to his as she took a step back, squeezing his shaft gently to indicate that he should follow. "I want you to lie down on the bed."

His eyes dropped to what she was doing to him as he followed her into the bedroom. She kept tugging on his stiff dick, pushing him closer to the edge with every stroke of her hand.

"Are you going to let me touch you as well?" Leith raised his gaze to catch her reaction to his question.

She shook her head with a smile on her face. "No, this is about you. I want to do something for you." A blush colored her cheeks, and she dropped her gaze. "But I like touching you, so I guess it's really for me too."

He wanted to touch her as well, but upon seeing the pleasure she was taking in touching him, he didn't want to push her. "Okay, but can I at least take off some of your clothes? I would love to see a little more of your skin while you have your wicked way with me."

She nodded and met his gaze. "I guess I can allow that." Her lips curved into a small smile. "Just remember that I'm going to be the one in control."

He narrowed his eyes at her in consideration. That Sabrina wanted to stay in control was nothing new, but maybe he could use that to show her he could handle her power. "I have one condition."

She narrowed her eyes right back at him. "Which is?"

"That you will use your power on me."

Her eyes widened in shock, and she snatched her hand away from his cock as if burned. "No! Absolutely not. I won't hurt you."

Leith gripped her upper arms and held her gaze. "I am not asking you to hurt me, Sabrina. I am asking you to give me a small pulse of your power to allow me to feel what it is like when it is directed at me. Do you remember what happened when you were using your power to locate Julianne? Feeling your power turned my cock as hard as stone, and I want to know if the same thing happens if you use your power on me and not just around me. You will be in control the whole time."

Staring at him, Sabrina visibly swallowed. "What if I hurt you? I'm not sure I'll be able to live with myself if I do."

He pulled her into his arms. Her body was tense with worry, but he held her close and spoke into her hair. "I don't think you will hurt me, and even if you do, it will be no more than I can handle. I heal exceptionally fast, even for a shifter."

She sighed before tipping her head back to stare up at him. "Okay, a small pulse. At least then you'll understand why I need to stay in control at all times."

Grinning at her, he gave her a nod. "Thank you. Can I undress you now?"

She chuckled, which was exactly what he had hoped for. "Okay, but my bra and panties stay on."

He gave her another nod. "If that is your wish."

Her shirt was soon gone, and he feasted his eyes on her smooth skin. Her breasts were partially hidden by her lacey bra, but he could make out her pink nipples through the thin fabric. She sucked in a breath when he cupped her soft breasts and brushed his thumbs lightly over her partially concealed nipples.

"Leith." His name left her mouth like a breath, before her hands came up and covered his, gently tugging them away from her breasts. "I need to stay in control, remember?"

"Does that mean I am not allowed to suck on your nipples?" Leith couldn't hide his grin as he watched desire add a warm glow to her blue eyes.

"Yes. That's exactly what it means. Now undress for me." Her eyes dipped to his still hard cock.

"But I have not even removed your pants yet." He made a show of licking his lips while he stared at the junction of her thighs.

She took a step back away from him like his closeness was affecting her more than she was comfortable with. "I'll do that while you take off your clothes."

CHAPTER 11

Leith quickly discarded his clothes until he was standing naked before her in all his glory. Sabrina had seen naked men before, but they paled in comparison to this man's male beauty. Every part of Leith was perfection. His lean yet muscular physique, his long, thick cock jutting proudly from between his legs, and his mesmerizing eyes, which at the moment shone emerald with desire.

She had removed her pants and was standing before him in nothing but a lacy bra and panties. His gaze was roving over her like he wanted to devour her, and she was certain that if his gaze had been anything like a caress, she would have felt him everywhere. Perhaps allowing him to see her almost naked hadn't been such a great idea. He had made it clear that he wanted her and that he didn't think her power was an issue, which left it up to her to make sure that this didn't get out of hand.

She squirmed under his intense gaze. It was turning

her on at an alarming rate. "You're staring."

A wicked grin spread across his face, and his eyes met hers. "Yes, I am enjoying the sight of my beautiful mate. It is something you should get used to because it will not be the last time I admire your body. But I intend to do much more than look at you from a distance when you let me. You deserve to be cherished and worshipped in every way, my angel, and I plan to spend the rest of my life doing exactly that."

She swallowed thickly, almost choking on his words. This wasn't what she needed to hear at the moment when she was already fighting to stay in control of her own desire. Maybe this had been a bad idea. "Leith, I—"

He didn't let her finish. "I know what you are going to say, Sabrina, but we will save that discussion for another day. Right now I am looking forward to whatever you are planning to do to me."

She pulled in a deep breath before letting it out slowly. "Then lie down on your back on the bed for me." The reason she had initiated this in the first place was to distract Leith from his bad reaction at Culloden. Or at least that was part of the reason. She also wanted to touch him and watch him come. Even if she couldn't give in to her own need, there was no reason he should wait to feel pleasure when she was more than happy to give it to him.

Leith kept his eyes on her while getting into position on the bed. When he was lying down like she had told him, she got on the bed by his feet and slowly crawled up over his body on her hands and knees until she was positioned directly above him. She lowered her head and brushed her lips against his before trailing kisses along his jawline.

A shiver ran through his body when she sucked on his earlobe. His hands came up and caressed her hips, causing her to back up slowly while kissing her way down to his chest. His touch was distracting, but she didn't want to tell him to remove his hands when she was soon going to move her body mostly out of his reach anyway.

She kissed across his chest until she reached one of his nipples. Using the tip of her tongue, she licked the small nub, and goosebumps pebbled his skin in response.

"If you are trying to tease me, you are doing a good job." Leith's voice was deep and scratchy, evidence that he liked what she was doing to him.

Smiling, she moved over to his other nipple and licked that one as well. "Good." She let her hands glide over his abs while she took her time kissing her way down toward his hard length. Wetness was soaking into her panties, and her clit was swollen and achy with the need to be touched, but there was nothing she could do about that. She'd just have to endure the pleasant torture while concentrating on Leith.

His body jerked when the head of his cock bumped against her chin. But she didn't pay the large appendage any attention. Instead, she let it slide against her cheek as she continued kissing down his belly.

"Sabrina." His voice was rough and trembling when he said her name. "Please touch me."

She chuckled against his skin at the plea in his tone. "I am."

"You know what I mean." There was a hint of desperation in his voice.

She lifted her head a little and met his hooded stare. His eyes were shining so bright they looked like they could burst into flame any second. Keeping her eyes on his, she stuck out her tongue and ran it smoothly from his base to his tip.

"Fuck!" Leith's eyes widened, and his whole body jerked so violently she had to catch herself not to fall off the bed. "That was—"

She wrapped her lips around his tip and sucked him into her mouth, and whatever he had been about to say died on his lips. Then, she suddenly remembered his condition. He wanted her to use her power on him.

After letting his cock slide from her mouth, she lifted her head to look at him. "Do you still want me to use my power on you?"

His gaze was on her mouth as he gave her a short nod. "Please."

"Okay." Putting her hands on his thighs, she sat down on his legs and kept her eyes on his face. Only one small pulse of her power. It might cause a second-degree burn to his skin, but that would be all. Taking a deep breath, she let a little of her power flow into him through her palms before quickly shutting it off.

Leith's roar took her completely by surprise, and she yanked her hands away from his skin to make sure she didn't hurt him more than she already had. One of his hands covered the head of his jerking cock as his body tensed beneath her, and she suddenly realized what was going on. He was coming. Hard.

Sabrina felt her jaw slacken in disbelief. This wasn't what she had expected to happen. Not at all. She had mentally prepared herself for causing him pain, but instead she had given him a powerful orgasm. And not by using her mouth on him like she had intended, but by letting him feel her power.

Leith was breathing hard when he opened his eyes to look at her. "That…" His voice broke, and he cleared his throat before starting again. "That was amazing. I did not expect it to be quite so…effective. Though, I was already close to coming by the time you used your magic."

She studied his face for any sign of discomfort before lowering her eyes to his thighs where she had touched him. His skin looked perfect without any blisters or redness to indicate he had been burned. "So, it didn't hurt at all?"

His chuckle brought her eyes back to his. "Did it look like I was in pain? I can assure you I was not. We will be doing that again, but the next time I want to be inside you when you use your power on me."

Pulling in a deep breath, she frowned at him. "I only used a small fraction of my power on you. This doesn't prove that you won't be hurt if I let you have a larger dose."

Leith gave her a single nod. "I understand that you do not want to hurt me, my angel. We can try this again several times using a gradual increase of your power if that is what it takes to convince you that you will not cause me any harm. Eventually, you will come to realize that you can let yourself go without worrying about me or other people nearby, because I will absorb your power." He sat up, and the corner of his mouth pulled up in a shadow of a smile. "I need to go clean up."

She moved off his legs to let him get off the bed. She stared at his tight ass as he moved toward the bathroom, and her mind felt like it was struggling to catch up with what had just happened. Was it possible that he was strong enough to take more of her power without any adverse effects? Based on her experience, it seemed like an impossibility, but her experience was formed from dealing with ordinary humans. And Leith was neither human nor ordinary. He had already shown that he could handle an amount of her power that would cause a human's skin to blister, and all it did was make him come. Not exactly an adverse effect.

Leith walked out of the bathroom a couple of minutes later, and her gaze automatically dropped to his groin. Her eyes widened when they landed on his hard shaft. "But you just…" Her eyes snapped up to his.

His expression was serious. "I still want you, Sabrina. Feeling your power was amazing, but it's you I want. To make love to you and watch you come on my cock."

"I…" Her voice died as her channel clenched in response to his words. She would like that too. Very much so.

Leith walked up to her and took one of her hands in his. When he pulled her gently toward him, she obliged and got off the bed to stand before him. Her hands were itching to touch him again, and she almost moaned when she remembered how his hard shaft had felt in her mouth.

Holding her gaze captive with his beautiful emerald orbs, he cupped her head gently before bending and slanting his lips over hers. She couldn't help the moan that escaped from her at the feel of his lips on hers.

He kissed her slowly and with more emotion than

before. It was a kiss more of love than of passion, and she could feel the barrier she had carefully constructed to keep anyone from getting too close, tearing slowly at the seams and falling away. She wanted this man more than anything else in the world, and for some crazy reason he wanted her as well. It might have been initiated by him realizing she was his mate, but there was no doubt anymore that he harbored feelings for her. And she already had feelings for him as well.

Slowly, he pulled away and stared down at her, and she almost gasped at the love shining in his eyes. "My mate. My beautiful and extraordinary mate. Nothing will ever be more important to me than you."

She wanted to tell him that he meant something to her as well, that she had feelings for him. But her tongue felt like it was stuck to the roof of her mouth all of a sudden, and she couldn't get any words out.

A phone rang in the living room, and it wasn't her ringtone. Leith sighed, and then brushed his lips over hers in a brief kiss before letting her go and striding out of the bedroom.

Sabrina just stood there, staring after him. This was all moving way too fast. Less than three days ago, she had resigned herself to a life without a significant other. And now she was falling for Leith, and her mind was even entertaining the possibility that they would be able to mate and spend their life together. She shouldn't let herself believe that, but it was too enticing an opportunity to discount it as impossible.

"She is right here. I will put you on speaker." Leith came back into the room and met her gaze. "It is Duncan and Julianne. I think they want to know whether you are okay staying with me." One of his eyebrows rose in question. "Are you?"

"I'm fine." A smile spread across her face as she answered.

"Are you sure?" There was a hint of concern in Julianne's voice. "I kind of feel like I abandoned you in the middle of our vacation."

Sabrina nodded. "Truly, I'm fine. Leith is doing his best to take care of me, while I'm doing my best to make it hard on him." Her gaze dropped to his groin, where his shaft was at half-mast. As she watched, his cock twitched and started swelling.

"What do you mean?" She could practically hear Julianne's concern through the phone. "Are you giving him a hard time?"

"Yes, I am." Sabrina grinned up at Leith and took a step toward him. "He's taking it well. But then I haven't been too mouthy yet." She reached out and gripped his hard length.

Leith's body tensed, and his eyes narrowed at her, but he didn't try to move away.

"Hmm." Julianne sounded like she was frowning heavily. "Why do I get the feeling your words have a double meaning?"

Sabrina laughed as she moved her hand slowly up and down Leith's erection. It was hard as stone beneath the velvety skin. "Can I call you back later, Julianne? Leith has just brought me something to eat." She squeezed his shaft gently and watched as his jaw slackened at her words.

"Oh. Okay. Talk to you later then."

CHAPTER 12

Leith ended the call as soon as Julianne's last word faded and put his phone on the desk behind him without looking. He was too busy staring into Sabrina's mischievous gaze. She had already told him what she intended to do to him, but he was a bit shocked that she had initiated it while on the phone with her friend. He had made the assumption that his mate was quite innocent and shy, but that was turning out not be the case. At least not entirely.

He was about to say something when she bent and wrapped her sweet lips around the tip of his cock, and whatever he had intended to say evaporated from his mind like morning dew in the sun. Her tongue flattened against his cock as she took more of him into her mouth, and he stared in fascination as her lips inched about halfway down his shaft before slowly pulling back.

It wasn't much more than ten minutes since he came, but he was already well on his way to another orgasm. It wouldn't take long with what his angel was doing to him. And one of the things that was pushing him toward the edge was the fact that Sabrina seemed to be enjoying what she was doing to him.

Her head bobbed slowly up and down as she used her tongue and lips to drive him crazy. His legs were threatening to give out beneath him as pleasure swirled through him, building quickly toward a climax of epic proportions. He took a small step backward, and then another, until he could sit down on the edge of the desk.

Sabrina let his cock slide from her mouth before looking up at him with a smile on her face. "Lie down on your back on the bed for me. I want to try something, but I'm not sure I can do it with you sitting."

"Okay." His voice was so rough it came out more like a low growl. He moved over to the bed and lay down, and as soon as he was on his back, Sabrina got into position above him. Her lips wrapped around his cock again, and he fisted the sheets to hold on against the onslaught of sensations.

She swirled her tongue around the head of his cock before sucking him into her hot mouth, and he all out growled as pleasure swirled through him. He expected her to stop when her lips reached about halfway down his shaft, but this time she didn't. She swallowed, and his cock continued down her throat until she had taken all of him.

Leith felt his eyes widen in disbelief and shear awe at the sight. He had never had a woman take all of him down her throat before, and it was by far the most erotic thing he had ever seen. She pulled back until only the tip was still in her mouth before swallowing him down again. And that was all it took. Ecstasy exploded through him as he started coming, roaring his pleasure as his shaft jerked with his release.

He gradually became aware of his surroundings and the warm body of his mate curled up next to him. His mind was officially blown. His mate was a goddess among women, but then he had already thought so before she sucked his cock down her throat. The only thing that would beat this was watching her come all over his cock, and he was getting impatient for that to happen.

"I think we have to leave soon if we're going to visit that wolfpack today." Sabrina spoke in a low voice next to his ear.

Leith sighed. He would have liked nothing better than to take his mate to a location far from other people where he could convince her to allow him to pleasure her. The need to mate her was growing stronger by the hour, but before they did that, he wanted a chance to focus on her and her pleasure. But none of that was going to happen in the next few hours. They had an evil witch to find.

He cleared his throat and turned his head to look at her. "I believe you are right." He turned onto his side and captured her lips in a firm kiss before pulling back. "Thank you, my angel, for giving me so much pleasure. I have never had anyone do to me what you just did." He grinned at her. "Taking my cock down your throat is the single most erotic thing I have ever experienced in my life, and I will not be opposed to you doing it again sometime."

A happy smile spread across her face. "So that was

a first for you?"

Nodding, he relished her happy smile. He wanted to see that smile on her face as often as possible in the future, and preferably with him being the reason it was there.

"Good. I thought you would've experienced it before since you're more than three hundred years old."

He smiled. "I have had my share of lovers over the years, and a couple have tried to swallow my cock. But since I am quite large, it was not a success."

Sabrina nodded. "Most people can't. Their gag reflex won't allow it. I don't know why I'm different. It's just never been an issue for me. But, I must admit that I wasn't sure I'd be able to since you're so big." Her expression sobered. "But we need to get ready, or we'll be late to our visit with the wolves."

Leith gave a short nod. "Yes, let us go. We can get something to eat on the way there."

∞∞∞∞

They were crossing the Kessock bridge, and Sabrina stared out over the water. According to Leith, the wolfpack was located less than an hour north of Inverness, so they were going to arrive on time. The meeting with the panther clan earlier in the day had been a bit of a shock due to their adherence to the rather old-fashioned shifter etiquette and their alpha's disrespectful pursuit of women, but Leith had assured her that Henry, the wolf alpha, was nothing like that. Normal human respect and courtesy was all he expected.

Sabrina turned toward Leith, taking in his profile as he kept his eyes on the road. She hadn't really considered his age before she saw his reaction at Culloden. The fact that he was alive when it happened was something she hadn't thought of when asking him to take her there.

She would have liked to ask him more questions about what actually happened back then, but after seeing his bad reaction, she wasn't sure it would be okay to do so. Making him relive that event might be considered cruel at the best of times.

"You're staring at me." Leith grinned and glanced at her. "I hope that's a good thing."

A smile curved her lips, and she felt the heaviness of her thoughts lift. "I like looking at you. You're a handsome man, Leith." Heat rose in her cheeks. She couldn't remember blushing like this since she was a teenager. "Actually, that's not correct."

"So not handsome, then?" Leith shot her another glance, and she noticed amusement in his eyes.

Swallowing, she tried again. "Yes. I mean no. You're more than handsome. That word doesn't do you justice. I'd rather call you gorgeous. Or irresistible like I've told you before."

"Thank you, my angel. I like that you think so." His grin was wide while he kept his eyes on the road. "I find you utterly irresistible as well, as I think you are already aware. And you are by far the most beautiful female I have ever met in my long life."

"Thank you." Sabrina didn't know what else to say. She'd had men fawn over her looks several times, but since none of them really mattered to her, their praise hadn't affected her like Leith's did.

They drove in silence for a while, and Sabrina's mind turned to the reason they were going to visit the wolfpack. Originally, the purpose of their visit was to tell the pack what they had recently discovered about Ambrosia. She was no longer just targeting alpha shifters, which meant that any unmated shifter was at risk.

However, based on Euna's information, they had another purpose as well. Someone in the wolfpack might be able to tell them more about Ambrosia, perhaps even give them her real identity, which would make finding her significantly easier.

There was one thing Sabrina didn't understand in all this, though. Why didn't Ambrosia just kill the alpha who mated her daughter against her will? It would have freed her daughter from the man who hurt her and held her captive. There was, of course, a chance that Ambrosia had tried killing him and failed, but it seemed unlikely based on what Sabrina had been told of the witch's power.

Sabrina was just opening her mouth to ask Leith about this when her heart almost jumped out of her mouth. At least that was what it felt like. Leaning back in her seat, she focused on her breathing while waiting for her heart to settle.

"Sabrina?" Leith's voice was filled with concern. "Are you in pain again?"

"No. My heart is racing. It's nothing to worry about." She gave him a reassuring smile, or at least what she hoped was a reassuring smile. Her face felt a bit stiff and unresponsive.

His face was a mask of worry when he glanced at her. "I'll find a place to pull over."

"No. Just keep driving. It will get better in a couple of minutes. It always does." Closing her eyes, she willed her heart to settle, but it kept slamming against her ribs like a small, terrified animal trying to get out of its cage.

Leith's hand touched her thigh, and it felt hot through her pants, making her realize how cold she was. Her body felt like she'd just plummeted into a tub of cold water.

As suddenly as it had started, the attack stopped. Her heartbeat evened out and settled at a normal, comfortable rate, and she sighed with relief.

She felt the car slow down and opened her eyes just as Leith pulled off the main road. He drove a couple of hundred yards before pulling onto the side and stopping.

The concern on his face when he turned to her made him look older than he usually did. "What can I do to help?"

Smiling, she shook her head. "Thank you, but it's already over. I'm fine now. Just a bit cold that's all."

"Come here." After unfastening her seatbelt, Leith gripped her upper arms and pulled her against him.

It was a bit awkward in the limited space of the car, but she forgot about that as soon as she felt his warmth against her. It felt amazing, and she burrowed into his embrace as best she could for maximum heat.

"When we mate, you will no longer have this issue. Any health issues you have will heal, and you will never suffer any illness again." There was a touch of anger in Leith's voice, but it seemed to be directed more at her heart condition than at her. She wasn't surprised at his reaction. He had already told her he was staying away from humans to avoid the pain when they suffered and died, and with her being his mate, she could only imagine how her health issues were affecting him.

"There's no need to worry about this." She lifted her head to stare up into his concerned face. "It's not a serious illness. Millions of people live with the same condition without any adverse effects. It has to be far more severe for the doctors to decide to do something about it."

Leith's eyes narrowed at her. "That does not mean it is not affecting you. I do not like it, and it only increases the importance of us mating as soon as possible."

She couldn't help chuckling at his concern. It seemed every human ailment was the same as a death sentence for this man. It was understandable with his history with humans and his inexperience with personal illness, but his concern was a bit out of proportion, considering her trivial issue. "I think you should save your concern for serious issues, and this isn't one of those."

His expression didn't change as he studied her face, perhaps looking for a sign that she was downplaying her condition. "I beg to differ. And the fact remains. Your health will become one hundred percent as soon as we mate. I am not sure I can let this go on for much longer."

That sounded an awful lot like he was going to force her to mate him, but Sabrina didn't think that was what he was trying to say. He wanted her to agree because he was genuinely concerned about her. It didn't mean she would agree before she was ready, though, and being ready included knowing she wouldn't hurt him or someone else when they mated.

She smiled up at him. "Let's discuss that when we get back from our meeting with the wolves. I'm feeling fine now, and we're late."

He gave her a short nod, but his expression was still one of concern as he slowly let her go. Sitting back in his seat, he waited for her to put on her seatbelt before he turned the car around.

CHAPTER 13

They pulled up in front of a large house situated at the end of a long driveway. A woman was sitting in a lounge chair on the porch, and her eyes followed their progress without fail since Sabrina noticed her. The woman would have been beautiful if not for the scowl on her face, and Sabrina got the impression it was a common expression for her.

They exited the car, and this time Leith didn't tell her to wait for him to open her door. It was obvious that their behavior wouldn't be judged based on old shifter etiquette by these wolves like it had been by the panthers.

As they approached the porch, a tall, lean man with flaming red hair stepped out of the house, and his face split into a wide grin when his eyes landed on Leith. "Leith. I was starting to think you had been held up." But based on the amusement in the man's hazel eyes, it didn't offend him that they were a bit late.

The corner of Leith's mouth pulled up in his typical

version of a smile as he stepped forward, and they gripped each other's forearm in greeting. "My apologies for being late, Henry. I hope that is not an issue."

"Not at all." Henry's gaze swung to Sabrina, and he gave her a warm smile. "And I see you've brought a guest. Welcome."

"Thank you." Sabrina gripped the man's extended hand in a firm handshake. Another sign that Henry had no problem with human customs.

"Please come inside." The wolf alpha swept his hand out in a clear invitation for them to enter the house ahead of him. Then, he turned to look at the woman sitting in the lounge chair. "Would you like to join us, Vamika?"

The woman gave a short nod and rose from her chair, before following them into the house.

Henry walked past them in the large hallway, and they followed him into a big office. It was tastefully decorated in light colors. Even the large desk was made of light wood. One end of the room was taken up by a huge beige leather corner sofa and two armchairs surrounding a low table. There was a tray with a thermos and cups in the middle of the table.

The alpha turned to face them. "I've made coffee, since I know Leith's preference for it. But if you'd like a cup of tea, Sabrina, I'd be happy to make that for you."

Smiling, Sabrina shook her head. "Coffee is perfect, Henry. Thank you."

"Okay. Then please sit down and have some coffee. I know why you're here, and I'm anxious to know more about this witch and the threat she's posing to shifters."

Leith moved around the table to sit on the couch, and Sabrina sat down next to him. Vamika waited until they had all sat down before she chose the armchair closest to the door. The scowl was still on her face like she didn't trust them, and it was going to take a lot to convince her otherwise.

***

Leith poured them both some coffee before he reached out and enveloped Sabrina's hand in his. He looked at Henry, who had taken a seat on the couch at the end of the table. "I mentioned when I first spoke to you that the witch was looking for an unmated alpha to use. Her promise was that she would use the mating bond to increase the alpha's power to a significantly higher level, and thereby make him a king among his kind. We do not know for sure how she intends to do this, or if indeed she even can, but we expect her goal is to gain more power for herself in the process."

Henry nodded while pouring his own coffee. "Yes, and I'm an unmated alpha, but I can promise you that I will never fall for her machinations."

"I know, Henry." Leith gave him a single nod. "You are not one of the alphas I am worried about. The thing is, Ambrosia does not seem to limit her potential candidates to alphas anymore. Just a few days ago, Sabrina's friend was close to being mated against her will to her ex-boyfriend, a panther shifter with a medium power level."

"Ambrosia?" Vamika's voice was low and smooth when she spoke, and it didn't seem to match the permanent scowl on her face.

"Yes." Nodding, Leith turned to look at the woman seated as far away from them as possible. "That is the name of the witch. Do you recognize the name?"

"Maybe." The woman paused like she was evaluating how much to tell them.

"Please tell us what you know, Vamika, even if it doesn't seem important." Henry nodded at her like he was trying to encourage her to share what she knew.

Vamika pulled in a deep breath before letting it out slowly. "Freddie tricked a human woman into mating him. Her mother came looking for her about a week after they mated, and the mother's name was Ambrosia. Freddie and his mate had already taken off by then. They'd moved out west somewhere. A few weeks later, he came by and told us that his mate had died, but he didn't want to say what had happened." She looked at Henry like she wanted him to elaborate.

The alpha wolf was frowning as he stared at Vamika. "So, you've met Mary's mother, and she was called Ambrosia? Why didn't you tell me, Vamika?"

Vamika shrugged. "You were in Inverness at the time, and she left as soon as I told her that they'd moved away. I probably should've told you, but then there was that fight between Dillon and his mate. I didn't remember until you mentioned her name just now." The woman's gaze swung to Leith.

"I see." Henry stared at the table for a few seconds before lifting his gaze to Leith. "This doesn't seem like a coincidence. Freddie convinced Mary to have sex with him, and then he mated her without her realizing what was going on and the significance of the act. He brought her back here and boasted about what he had done. He even went so far as to encourage others to do the same. Needless to say, I came down on him hard. It took him a couple of days to recover from the beating I gave him. I knew he was an asshole, but even I hadn't expected him to do something like that.

"Mary was livid and made no secret of the fact that she hated his guts for what he had done to her. I let them stay in the hopes that Mary would settle into her new life with the help of the women here, but they only stayed for a few days after Freddie recovered before they left. I considered going after them, but I didn't. This is a pack, not a prison. Any pack member is free to leave if they so choose."

Sabrina leaned forward, and there was confusion on her face when she spoke. "I'm not sure I understand. Did Freddie keep this woman tied up or threaten her with violence? From what you've just told us, it almost sounds like she chose to stay with him. I don't understand why she didn't leave him as soon as she realized what he had done."

Henry looked surprised at Sabrina's words, and Leith realized he hadn't told her enough about how a mating bond worked. "I am sorry, my angel. I have obviously neglected to tell you how a mating bond works. Once you are mated, you are bonded for life, even if you are not true mates, but the consequences can be positive or negative, depending on whether you are mated to a person you care about and respect or not. The bond will pull you together no matter your feelings for your mate, and staying away from your mate will be painful. Leaving your mate is a physical impossibility for most people, and if your mate suddenly dies, then you will die shortly after. It is rare if someone is able to live without their mate for more than a week."

Sabrina was staring at him with her mouth open like he had just told her he was the creator of the universe. But perhaps what he had just told her qualified as just as crazy for someone who was new to the shifter world. Quite a few humans treated marriage and divorce like nothing special, and he would imagine that a mating bond would scare most of them half to death.

Sabrina shook her head like she was trying to clear her mind. "So, let me get this straight. There is no way to dissolve a mating? Not even if it happened accidentally or was done without your consent?" Her eyes were narrow when she stared at him.

Leith nodded. "That is correct, and it is the reason why mating is a serious decision among shifters. Unless you find your true mate. Then, the decision is usually a simple one. I thought you already knew this, since your friend Julianne mated Duncan, but I realize that I should not have made that assumption. You have only known about shifters for a few days. I am sorry for not telling you sooner. It would have been the appropriate thing to do."

She nodded slowly before her gaze dropped to her lap. "Yes, it would have been."

Leith felt his whole body tense with trepidation. Sabrina was clearly shocked by what he had just told her, and rightly so. He should have made sure she knew, but with everything that had happened the last few days, and his own amazement that he had found his true mate at last, a lot of what she needed to know was still left unsaid. He would have to rectify that as soon as possible. At least she hadn't pulled her hand from his. He chose to take that as a sign that she was going to forgive him for not telling her more about mating bonds.

Henry cleared his throat discretely. "Do you want some time to yourself for a while?"

Taking a deep breath, Leith swung his gaze to the other man. "I—"

"No." Sabrina's voice was clear and strong. "Leith and I can talk about this later. Let's continue."

Henry gave a single nod of acknowledgement. "If Mary's mother and the witch you're looking for is one and the same, there's no doubt why she's using shifters to gain power."

"Revenge." Leith nodded. "Yes, we have considered that as well."

Henry's eyes narrowed in thought. "But if that's the case, I find it unlikely that her promise of power to a shifter during mating is anything but a ruse. She will use the mating to gain power for herself, and I'm not so sure it will be a positive experience for the mates. They may end up hurt or even dead in the process."

Leith stared at the alpha wolf. This was something they hadn't considered, but now that Henry mentioned it, it seemed a logical conclusion. "We never thought of that. We always assumed that Ambrosia would gain the most power from the mating, but that the shifter would gain enough power to become the strongest of his kind. That way Ambrosia would gain control of a shifter kind through its strongest member. He would be indebted to her for enabling him to become the supreme alpha, so to speak. But I think you may be right. She will not allow anyone else to gain power but herself, and if she can destroy shifters through the very mating bond that took her daughter, that is a form of justice served."

Henry nodded. "Yes, a horrible form of justice, and I can't imagine that she will stop until she feels justice has been served, and who knows how much damage she's done by then. Hurting innocents doesn't deter her, which means she's beyond redemption. She has to be destroyed. It's the only way to stop her in my opinion."

"I agree." Leith sighed. Taking a life wasn't something he relished, but desperate times and so on. "But first we have to find her, and that is proving difficult, since we have not been able to establish her real identity."

"What did Mary's mother look like?" Sabrina's voice made Leith turn to look at her. She was looking at Vamika. "I've never seen her myself, but Julianne described her to me."

Vamika narrowed her eyes in thought. "Green eyes and long reddish-gold hair. She was elegantly dressed but a little disheveled like she hadn't paid attention when she dressed that morning. Not surprising, I guess, if she was worried about her daughter."

Sabrina nodded. "Sounds like the same woman. Where is Freddie now? Do you know?"

Vamika shrugged, and Sabrina swung her gaze to Henry.

Henry pulled in a deep breath before letting it out on a sigh. "I don't know, and to be honest it would surprise me if he's still alive. He came by to tell us that Mary was dead, and then he left without answering any of our questions. We don't know whether he killed her by accident, or she took her own life. My guess is the latter."

"You do not think he killed her intentionally?" Leith kept his expression neutral as he stared at Henry.

"No." The alpha wolf shook his head. "By the time they left the pack, Freddie was so affected by the mating bond that he was acting like a lovesick puppy. Mary didn't seem to be that affected, though, and was keeping him at an arm's length whenever I observed them. That's why I think there's a chance he killed her by accident, but with the way he was acting, I don't think he would be able to kill her outright. But of course, I could be wrong. Who knows what happened after they left the pack. The only reason we know that they lived out west is because Freddie told us when he came by after Mary was dead. We don't even know what he did with her body."

Leith nodded. "What was Mary's full name?"

A sad expression spread across Henry's face. "I don't even know that. I tried talking to her on more than one occasion, but she either told me to fuck off or just walked away without acknowledging me at all. In that respect she was like Freddie. He didn't have a pleasant personality either. You might think that her attitude was a result of what Freddie did to her, but I got the feeling she was like that from before. What Freddie did, only accentuated her bad personality traits."

"Do you think she told anyone else who she was or any other details about herself that could give us a clue as to her identity?" Leith looked at Henry before moving his gaze to Vamika.

Vamika shook her head. "I never talked to her."

"I don't think she talked to anyone." Henry sighed.

"But I can ask around just to make sure and send you a text if anyone knows anything. I wouldn't hold my breath, though."

"Okay." Leigh nodded. "Thank you, Henry and Vamika, for taking the time to talk to us. At least we have established that Ambrosia is Mary's mother. That is something."

"Always happy to help, Leith." Henry smiled. "I'll get in touch if I see or hear anything that might be relevant to finding the witch. In the meantime I'll try to keep my wolves safe from her. And please tell me if there's anything we can do to help in your search."

"Thank you, Henry." Leith rose from the sofa, and Sabrina got up as well. Her hand was still in his, which was a comfort since he had upset her with not making sure she knew more about what mating entailed. They had some talking to do when they got back to the hotel.

CHAPTER 14

Sabrina walked into their suite ahead of Leith. The drive back had been a bit awkward with silence reigning between them. But she didn't want to start asking questions about the mating bond while Leith was driving. It was a discussion better had when they both could give it their undivided attention.

"Sabrina." Leith's voice sounded from behind her, and she turned to see him standing just inside the closed door, watching her. "We need to talk."

Nodding, she met his gaze. "We do. Let's sit down." She went to the couch and sat down.

Leith studied her for a second before he moved across the room. He sat down next to her, their bodies an inch from touching.

Sabrina almost told him to move. His close proximity was affecting her, and she wanted to maintain a clear head through their talk. She was falling for Leith, there was no doubt about that, and no matter what the mating bond entailed, she didn't think she'd be able to keep her distance for long. And after what happened earlier between them, she even entertained a tiny hope that they would be able to mate without Leith being severely injured in the process.

Leith sighed. "Please accept my apologies, Sabrina. I—"

She didn't let him finish. He had already apologized enough. "It's okay, Leith. I probably should've realized that it worked like that. You've already told me that the mating bond will start taking effect even before the actual mating, and that human mates will live as long as their shifter partners. I just never equated that with the fact that you can never live separately again. It never crossed my mind that the bond could be that powerful and irreversible."

"It is extremely powerful, and even more so for true mates." Leith reached over and put his hand on top of one of hers. "What I said, about the mating bond starting to develop before the mating, is true for true mates only. Other couples can feel affection for each other before mating, but the mating bond does not take effect before they have mated."

Sabrina was still blown away by all this. Talk about being thrown into a whole new life. The world had radically changed in less than a week, even with her already knowing about witches. "So I guess I don't have a choice about becoming your mate."

Leith's hand tensed where it rested over hers. "Is that so bad? I thought you liked me, and that it was your fear of hurting me and others that was preventing you from mating me."

She pulled in a deep breath before letting it out on a sigh. "I like you, Leith, but it all feels so inevitable. I'm a pragmatic person, but this mating bond thing is a bit too unromantic even for me. It would've been nice to feel that you actually want to be with me, and it's not just your shifter nature that's decided your fate for you."

Leith's hand disappeared from hers when he turned toward her. He gripped her upper arms, and his gaze was intense when he captured hers. "That is not how this is. I want you with everything I am. Nothing and nobody are more important to me than you. And I have feelings for you, strong feelings for you, making my heart swell with love and pride whenever I touch you or look at you. I cannot promise you that I would have fallen in love with you if the bond had not shown me who you were, but I dare say that I would. A true mate is not some random person. It is the person who is a perfect match for you in every way. It does not mean that true mates never disagree or get angry with each other, but it means that the love and companionship can be a lot better than anything you could hope to have with any other person."

Sabrina was stunned by Leith's intensity and words. He loved her? That was much too soon surely. Her mind was scrambling for a response to his speech, but it was like her brain was malfunctioning, and she couldn't come up with anything to say.

Leith slowly pulled her closer before wrapping his arms around her. And she buried her face against his warm, solid chest. It felt so amazing being in his arms, like she had come home after a long journey. But she wasn't quite sure whether to be happy about that or not. This whole thing was crazy, and even though a part of her was pushing her to accept it and jump in with both feet without delay, another part, the sane and controlling part, was telling her to take a step back and consider the consequences thoroughly before proceeding with caution.

Leith's ringtone started playing, and he swore under his breath. He let go of her and pulled his phone out of his pocket.

"Duncan." Leith didn't sound happy, and a heavy frown marred his face. He put the phone on speaker and held it out between them.

"Did I catch you at a bad time?" There was amusement in Duncan's voice, and Sabrina found herself smiling despite the lingering seriousness between her and Leith.

She spoke before Leith had a chance to respond. "No, you didn't, Duncan. It's wonderful to hear your cheerful voice."

"Ah, Sabrina. Did you miss me?" Duncan's question was followed by a yelp and some mumbled words from Julianne.

Sabrina laughed. "You and Julianne both, yes. Although Leith's seriousness is growing on me." She smiled as she met his astonished gaze.

"I am not that serious." The frown was back on his face like he wasn't sure what to make of her change in mood.

She reached out and put a hand on his cheek. "No, you can be fun as well." Smiling, she watched as the corner of his mouth pulled up in a small smile.

A squeal sounded through the phone before Julianne spoke. "Oh, I think she's falling for him. You're falling for him aren't you, Sabrina?"

Sabrina laughed. Julianne sounded like a fourteen-year-old. "Maybe."

Before she realized what he intended, Leith cupped the back of her head with one hand, leaned in, and crushed a kiss to her lips before letting her go. It was so sudden that Sabrina didn't have time to react before it was over.

"That was a kiss. I know it was." Julianne's excited voice sounded over the phone. "He just kissed her."

Leith grinned at her and nodded. "I did, and it might take a few seconds before she finds her voice again."

Duncan and Julianne's laughter sounded through the phone, and Sabrina felt her cheeks heat, even though they couldn't see her and she had witnessed them flirting and kissing several times.

"Now, why are you bothering us?" Leith's eyes were on hers as he spoke. "I hope you have a good reason."

"Actually we do." The previous amusement in Duncan's voice was gone. "Callum has been trying to identify Ambrosia's phone based on her known movements since he joined us yesterday. It's been tricky since we only know where she's been on three specific days, and two of those days, she was staying at Jack's estate where no cell phones are allowed. Even so, he's been able to narrow it down to three separate numbers.

"They're all registered to a woman, they were all in Fort Augustus at the same time Steven was there, and they were all turned off or out of range at the time Ambrosia was staying at the estate with Jack. And last but not least, we've not been able to rule them out for other reasons. Whoever uses these phones doesn't use them much, and they are often turned off, but the reason we're calling is that one of them was just turned on in Inverness. We've tried calling the number, but nobody's answering. We don't know that this is Ambrosia's phone, but it's a one in three chance that it is. Unless she doesn't have a phone at all."

The frown was back on Leith's face. "You should check the phone records and see if one of the women has been calling a Mary regularly about five or six months ago. Ambrosia's daughter was called Mary, and she was mated against her will to an alpha in Henry's pack. You remember the alpha who killed his mate a few weeks after mating her? That was Mary, and it has not been confirmed whether she was killed or chose to take her own life."

"Fuck!" Duncan sounded shocked. "No wonder Ambrosia is fucking with shifters. If one of them killed her daughter… I'll tell Callum about Mary so he can do his magic with that information. If it turns out Ambrosia's in Inverness, we'll probably all be heading in your direction soon."

"Good." Leith's gaze was on Sabrina as he spoke. "It would be good to have backup when we confront her. I do not want to put Sabrina in more danger than necessary. If I had my way, she would take no part in this at all, but I do not think she will heed my opinion in this."

"No, I won't." Sabrina narrowed her eyes at him. "I'm better equipped to handle this woman than most of you, considering I'm a witch. And I won't accept everyone else putting themselves at risk without me. I'd rather confront her alone if that was an option, but I don't think it is."

"No, it is not." Leith's eyes were narrow with anger. "We will confront her together or not at all. Nothing else is acceptable."

A smile spread across her face in response to his words. It felt good to have a man who made it clear he was going to stand by her no matter what. And he wasn't the least bit scared of her powers or apprehensive of what she was.

Laughter sounded through the phone. "If it's any consolation, I don't think I'll be able to keep Julianne out of this either, and she doesn't even have magic to protect herself. She has agreed to stay in the background, though. Thank fuck. Or I might've had to tie her up somewhere safe."

"You could've tried. Just remember that I will attack that bitch if she hurts you." It was easy to hear Julianne's anger in her voice. She wasn't happy with the prospect of having Duncan in the line of fire.

Sabrina sighed. This confrontation wasn't something she looked forward to. And unfortunately, she was sure there would be a confrontation. "We'll have to come up with a plan before we approach Ambrosia. Rushing into this is a recipe for disaster. But let's discuss that when you get here. If you get here. We don't know where Ambrosia is yet."

"We'll get in touch as soon as we know more." Duncan sighed. "Hopefully that will be soon. I'd like to get this over and done with so I can take my mate on a proper honeymoon."

They said their goodbyes, and Sabrina suddenly became aware of how close she was to Leith and that they didn't have any plans for the evening.

Leith's eyes started glowing, indicating that

something similar had occurred to him. And before she knew what was happening his lips was on hers, and her body was heating with a desire that threatened to take her breath away.

She wrapped her arms around his neck and pressed her body against his as tightly as she could, considering they were sitting next to each other on the couch. Their tongues were sparring and dueling, and she moaned into his mouth when her channel clenched with insistent need.

Large, strong hands grabbed her thighs, and a second later she was sitting on Leith's lap with her pussy firmly pressed against his erection. She moaned into his mouth as another stronger wave of need rolled through her, forcing her to rock her hips and grind herself against his hard length. Her channel clenched, and wetness soaked into her panties. She had never felt such an overwhelming desire to be filled in her life. It was threatening to rob her of all her usual control and make her abandon her sanity in order to feel Leith's long, thick cock force its way inside her and satisfy her aching need.

Leith put his hands on her ass and pressed her even tighter against him as he started rolling his hips. She gasped and shuddered as her swollen clit was rubbed hard against him, causing pleasure to build like heat in her lower belly as a promise of what was to come.

Sabrina ripped her mouth away from his, and he opened his eyes to stare at her with glowing emerald orbs. "Leith. I want—" Her words were cut off as Leith had her on her back on the couch in one swift move. His body was on top of hers with his lower body cradled between her thighs. His mouth covered hers, and his hips moved to create just the right amount of friction against her clit.

All thoughts disappeared and her body took over. Her hands locked onto his head, their kissing turning frantic as need drove their actions.

Her hips rocked against his in desperation for the climax hovering just out of reach. It felt so good giving in to her desire, and she couldn't remember why she hadn't done it before. They should get rid of their clothes so they could do this properly, but there was no time. She wanted that release immediately, everything else could wait.

Leith adjusted his position slightly and drove his hard cock against her pussy. Everything tightened. Her channel clenched hard, and pleasure erupted from her center like a volcano, sending molten heat through her veins and igniting every cell of her body. She screamed as wave after wave of pleasure crashed through her.

Leith's body stiffened, and he roared so loudly Sabrina's breath seized in her chest. Her orgasm died in an instant, and her whole body went cold with dread. *No!* She had just done exactly what she knew she couldn't. And she had hurt him. Badly.

"Leith." She lifted her hands from his shoulders and looked at the shirt covering his skin. Carefully, she pulled his shirt away from one of his shoulders and studied his skin. It was red, but there were no blisters. Perhaps he wasn't as badly hurt as she had thought, but he had yet to respond to her.

"Leith!" His chin was resting on her shoulder, and his face was hidden from her sight. She gripped his head with both hands and lifted it until she could see his face. His eyes opened slowly to reveal pulsing emerald orbs not quite able to focus.

"Oh, Leith. I'm so sorry. I—"

"Stop." The word was slurred. "Not hurt."

She felt herself frowning. Did he mean what it sounded like? "You're not hurt?"

"Not hurt." He blinked his eyes a few times before he focused on her. His eyes were hooded, and she watched a devastating grin spread across his face. "But my pants are wet."

She snorted with relief. "You came."

"Harder than I ever have. Fuck, woman. I think I will have to take you to bed and stay there for a very long time." He leaned in and brushed his lips slowly against hers before pulling back to grin at her again.

"I thought I'd hurt you severely this time." Smiling at him, she carefully removed the hair tie from his hair before burying her fingers in his long, thick copper-colored tresses.

"You seem to think that a lot." He leaned in and gave her a slow kiss before pulling away. "Stop worrying about me, my angel. You have not been able to hurt me yet, and I doubt you ever will."

"Don't say that." She stared into his beautiful emerald gaze. She had expected the color of his eyes to start changing back to their usual dark green, but they hadn't yet. "You still haven't been subjected to a full blast of my power. I gave you a significantly higher doze now than I did earlier today, but if the intensity of mating is anywhere near what the other women have described, then I fear what will happen."

"So no mating today, is that what you are telling me?" There was seriousness in his voice, but a small smile curved his lips.

"Yes." She nodded. "That's a chance I'm not willing to take until I know you can handle it without pain or injury, or I learn how to control my power during an extreme situation like that. But I'm starting to doubt that the latter will ever be possible for me."

"Well, in that case there is only one thing to do." Leith's wicked grin made her frown with suspicion.

"And what's that?"

Leith quickly rose from the couch, and then she was in his arms as he carried her toward the bedroom. "We will have to practice to make sure I can handle your power without any ill effects."

Her channel clenched in response to his words. She had come hard, but it had been cut short, and apparently, her body was eager for more. "I… Are you sure that's wise so soon after I hit you with my power? Maybe we should wait a while to let you recover."

He grinned down at her. "I have recovered, and I am ready for more. Are you? I want to taste you."

Sabrina felt her jaw slacken, and a shiver ran through her at the image he put in her head. She had never let anyone go down on her before. It was one of the things she had avoided to make sure she didn't have an orgasm and accidentally hurt someone. "Okay." Her voice was husky with her need, and Leith's grin widened.

He put her down on her feet next to the bed. "I need to clean up a bit."

Sabrina's gaze dropped to his groin, and she wasn't surprised to see a large wet patch covering the front of his pants. What did surprise her, though, was the outline of his hard cock straining against the fabric. There was no doubt that he was ready for a round two as also evidenced by his emerald eyes.

"I will be right back." He turned away from her and headed toward the bathroom. "I expect you to be naked on the bed by the time I get back."

Her jaw dropped at his command, and more of her wetness seeped into her panties. She didn't usually like to be told what to do, but for some reason, Leith's words made her clit throb in anticipation of his attention.

Without delay she discarded her clothes in a pile on the floor and climbed onto the bed. She had just laid down on her back when Leith emerged from the bathroom. He was naked, and his thick shaft was standing proud from between his legs.

"Good girl." Smiling, he let his gaze wander slowly from her feet to her face, and the heat in his eyes made her squirm with need.

He moved to the foot of the bed, grabbed her ankles, and proceeded to pull her toward him until her ass was resting on the edge of the bed. Kneeling on the floor between her legs, he moved his gaze to zone in on her sex, and Sabrina felt heat rising in her cheeks. She had never had a man stare at her pussy like that. It was a bit unnerving and embarrassing, even though it shouldn't be. She had already sucked his cock, and now he wanted to return the favor. There was no reason to be embarrassed.

A finger slipped between her folds, and she jerked in response. She was drenched, and his finger slid easily up to her clit and over it, making her shudder with the intensity of the sensation.

"Beautiful and so wet. You are perfect." Leith's gaze was still on her pussy as he spoke. "I will enjoy playing with you, my angel. Very much so." His gaze lifted to hers, and his wicked smile made her want to kiss him.

Using both hands, he parted her folds. The look on his face as he studied her made her feel like he was appraising a piece of art he was intending to buy. Or perhaps appreciating a piece he had already bought and wanted to enjoy to the fullest.

His head lowered, and his tongue started playing along the edges of her slit. Slowly, he moved upward toward her clit, and Sabrina could feel her eyes widen with anticipation. She wanted his tongue on her swollen pleasure button more than anything else she could think of. But just before his tongue reached her clit, he changed directions and licked a circle around her throbbing nub. A groan of disappointed escaped her.

Leith chuckled against her pussy, and she gasped at the vibration. Sabrina didn't think she had ever been this turned on with hardly any direct stimulation. Her body felt tense with pent-up desire, and she wanted to grab Leith's head and direct his mouth to where she wanted him.

"Would you like me to play with your clit?" Leith's mouth was hovering a hair's breadth from her sensitive nub as he gazed up at her. His eyes were filled with mischief, evidence that he knew precisely how desperately she wanted him to do exactly that.

"Please." Her voice was needy and sounded weird in her own ears. "I need your tongue on me."

The last word had barely escaped her lips before he sucked her clit into his mouth, and her back arched off the bed as she screamed her approval. "Yes! Oh, yes."

Leith chuckled again, and the vibration forced another scream from her lungs. Pleasure was gathering like a hot ball low in her belly, and she squeezed her eyes shut as her channel clenched and begged to be filled.

Before she could tell this amazing man what she needed, she felt a finger breach her entrance and push inside her. She moaned as her internal walls clenched around his finger, her body desperate to keep him inside her. Then, he added a second digit and started finger-fucking her while he sucked on her clit.

Frantic screams and mewling noises were forced from her as he pushed her closer to orgasm with every suck and thrust.

He suddenly let go of her swollen nub, and she groaned in protest. Opening her eyes, she narrowed them in accusation as she met his gaze, ready to tell him off for leaving her hanging.

"Put your hands on my shoulders, Sabrina. I want to feel your power when you come."

She did as she was told, and no sooner did she grip his shoulders than he started vibrating his tongue against her sensitive nub while he kept thrusting his fingers into her. It was too much, and she tried to wriggle away from him, but he put an arm around her hips and held her in place without stopping what he was doing with his tongue and fingers.

CHAPTER 15

Leith would have laughed at her amazing sounds and her wriggling to get away from his tongue if his mouth wasn't busy. He knew he was pushing her rapidly toward another orgasm, and he wasn't going to let up until she screamed her pleasure. Taking it slowly might give her time to have second thoughts about hitting him with more of her power so shortly after last time, and he wasn't going to allow her the opportunity to say stop. Not when saying stop would be because she was worried about him. There was no reason for her to be concerned about him, and sustaining a second dose of her potent power within a short time would prove that to her.

"Leith, it's too much. I..." Her tight channel clamped down on his fingers with surprising force a second before she screamed with the power of her orgasm.

Her power slammed into him with a force like a locomotive, almost throwing him backward. Somehow he managed to stay where he was with his mouth on her clit even as her magic raced through him. Pleasure even more powerful than last time exploded through him, and he roared against her sensitive flesh as his seed shot from his cock like cannon fire. The intense pleasure kept pulsing through him until his balls were running on empty and his lungs were working overtime.

It took him a while for his pleasure-overloaded brain to stop misfiring and start connecting with his body again. Lifting his head from where it was resting on Sabrina's belly, he met her worried blue gaze. "I am fine," he croaked and tried to give her a convincing smile, but he wasn't sure his grimace and cross-eyed stare was reassuring at all.

Sabrina sat up, and her hands cupped his face as she stared into his eyes. "Are you sure? You look like you accidentally touched a high voltage source."

"Perhaps I did." He let the love he was feeling for this perfect woman show in his eyes. "Your magic is an amazing force. I think I might have fallen in love with it." Staring into her eyes, he gave her what he hoped was a teasing smile.

The worry left her eyes, and she smiled back at him. "Thank you, Leith. I've never had anyone do that to me before."

"You mean lick that pretty pussy of yours?" He licked his lips for emphasis.

Her gaze dropped to his mouth. "Yes." She closed the distance between them and put her lips on his in a gentle and slow kiss.

He put his arms around her and let his hands play along her spine while they shared lingering kisses. No words were necessary at the moment. Sabrina's kisses were saying what she hadn't formulated with words yet, and happiness surged through him like a different kind of magic, making his future brighter and more promising than it had ever been. There were so many amazing moments to come, and he was going to share them all with his angel.

They broke apart slowly, and Leith breathed out a sigh of contentment. They had taken a huge step toward mating, and he was convinced it would be no more than a couple of days before they could take the final step. Which was good, because his body had been ready since he first laid eyes on Sabrina two days before, and even though a couple of days wasn't enough to get to know each other very well, it was enough for his body to start pestering him about what he needed to do.

Not many shifters were lucky enough to find their true mate, and for those who did, their true mate was usually a shifter. They didn't need time to adjust or accept what was happening between them, and consequently, they mated as soon as possible. There was no hesitation, since they knew they were lucky, and mating would bind them together and allow them to get to know each other faster.

But with a human mate, it didn't work the same. They might feel the mating bond, but it was natural for them to resist the feeling because they didn't want to tie themselves to someone they didn't know yet. It put a strain on the shifter since their bodies didn't understand waiting, but their minds understood that pushing someone into making a life-changing decision in a couple of days was extreme.

Leith was determined to wait until Sabrina was ready, but he realized he was only going to be able to fight his body for control for so long. That didn't mean he would mate her against her will, but it might mean he would push her harder and be much more demanding in his quest to mate her. Hopefully, they would mate before it came to that, because that kind of behavior might push her away rather than pull her closer. In the end she probably wouldn't be able to resist the mating bond, either, but by then something precious might already have been destroyed between them.

"Your mind seems to be somewhere else." Sabrina's voice penetrated his thoughts, and he realized he'd been in his own mind for a while and had not paid attention to her at all.

"I am sorry." He cupped her cheek. "Just thinking about what is happening between us."

She frowned. "Based on your expression, it didn't look like happy thoughts."

He sighed and let his hand skim the side of her face and down to the base of her throat. "Both yes and no. The fact that I have found you fills me with a joy that is more intense than I have ever experienced. At the same time, my body is driving me to claim you as my mate, and it is getting more insistent with every passing hour. It is only a question of time before it will affect my mood and behavior, but it does not mean that I do not respect your choice to wait or your reasons for that choice. If I get short-tempered and pushy, please do not let that drive a wedge between us. I do not know all the ways in which my need to mate you will affect me, but I hope it will not scare you and cause you to pull away from me. This worries me."

Taking a deep breath, Sabrina gave him a small smile. "You might turn into a pushy, growly, horny beast. Is that what you're telling me?"

He gave her a short nod. "I think that sums it up well."

"Will sucking your cock help?" Her smile broadened into a grin.

He chuckled at her enthusiasm. "I wish I could say that it will, but I am not so sure. Perhaps it will provide some temporary relief, but I do not think it will last long."

Sabrina's smile faded as she stared at him. "How long do you think we have before your mood will be affected?"

Leith shrugged. He didn't have any firsthand experience with a mating bond, but based on some of Trevor's comments, he didn't think he had long. "Not long. Maybe a day. Hopefully, more."

"A day." Her eyes had widened in surprise. "I guess I shouldn't be surprised after watching how Julianne and Duncan couldn't keep their hands off each other." A thought seemed to cross her mind. "Will you be in pain?"

"Perhaps after a couple of days or so. My body will be constantly turned on with everything that entails. I imagine it will get uncomfortable after a while."

Sabrina narrowed her eyes at him. "I don't like that, but I can't risk severely hurting you. It's promising that you can handle my power to the extent you have so far, but I'm afraid it's nowhere near what you will have to sustain when we mate."

Leith nodded slowly. "I know you worry about that,

my angel, and even though I believe I can handle it, I cannot prove that to you without you actually using your power on me. But let us not worry about that tonight. I think we have made significant progress since this morning. We should go out and get something to eat before we turn in for the night. We have an early start tomorrow. The pack we are going to visit is close to the northernmost tip of mainland Scotland, and it will take us more than two hours to get there."

CHAPTER 16

Sabrina turned to Leith as they entered their hotel suite. Leith was good at picking restaurants, and they had shared a fantastic meal together.

She was starting to feel more comfortable around him. Not that things had been constantly awkward between them before, but having sex earlier and experiencing that she didn't have to hold off her own orgasm to protect him had let her relax more around him and enjoy his company and attention.

She was just opening her mouth to tell him her thoughts when his phone rang.

Leith pulled it out of his pocket and put it on speaker. "Callum, how are you doing?"

"Good thanks, Leith. Yourself?" Callum's pleasant voice sounded through the phone.

"Close to perfect, I think." Leith's gaze met hers, and a smile curved his lips.

A deep chuckle reached them. "Sounds good. I have some good news. Well, it's good if you're looking to catch an evil witch, not so good if you would like time for yourself."

Leith narrowed his gaze. "I am guessing you know where Ambrosia is."

"Correct. She's in Inverness, and we're on our way there now."

Leith nodded. "We, as in Duncan and Julianne are with you?"

"Yes. Duncan's driving, so we'll probably be there in a couple of hours. We've booked rooms at the hotel you're staying at. Will you join us for breakfast tomorrow?"

Leith nodded as he met Sabrina's gaze. "Yes, we were going to go visit the pack far north tomorrow, but I will call to postpone since we know where Ambrosia is. If we can corner her here and put a stop to this mess, we can all go back to our normal lives."

"Yes." There was a smile in Callum's voice. "There are a couple of people in this car who hope to be spending more time alone together, and I'm not one of them."

Laughter and affirmative exclamations could be heard in the background from the car.

Sabrina smiled at Leith and nodded. She wouldn't mind some time alone with this man, preferably far from people, where they could test possible ways of mating without Leith absorbing too much of her power. She didn't like that he might end up being in pain before they could mate due to his body's need to claim her as his.

"We will see you tomorrow morning then. Around eight?" Leith raised an eyebrow at Sabrina in question, and she nodded her agreement.

"Eight's fine. See you then." Callum ended the call.

Leith put the phone away and took a step toward her. Grabbing her hands, he stared into her eyes. "So will you allow me to sleep with you tonight?"

Sabrina laughed. "Will you allow me to get some sleep, or will you keep me up all night with other activities?"

A wicked smile spread across Leith's face and made her question her own teasing. The man was too gorgeous for his own good, or perhaps her own good. She was never going to get any sleep if he tempted her with his wicked smile, fantastic body, and sinful mouth.

"You might sleep better if I wear you out first. Have you considered that?" He leaned in and brushed a soft kiss against her lips before pulling back with a serious expression on his face. "Then again you need a full night's sleep. If we find Ambrosia tomorrow, there is a good chance there will be an altercation, and I do not want you at risk because you are tired."

Sabrina couldn't help chuckling at his sudden seriousness. "First you temp me with your promise of passion, and then you tell me to sleep. Are you trying to punish me? Because in that case, it's working."

He narrowed his eyes at her and sighed in frustration. "Your safety is important, more important than sex. I can easily forgo sex to ensure your safety."

"Okay." She shrugged like it didn't matter to her. "I'll go get ready for bed, then." Turning away from him, she kept her face blank. She wasn't going to let him off that easily, but he didn't need to know that yet.

Sabrina brushed her teeth and went to the toilet, but she didn't undress in the bathroom. She had a plan, and it would be interesting to see how fast Leith would fall into her trap.

Leith was sitting on the bed fully clothed when she exited the bathroom. She met his gaze and started slowly unbuttoning her shirt. "Will you sleep here in the bed with me tonight, or have you changed your mind about that as well? I'm not sure I'll be able to stay away from you if you're next to me."

His eyes were on her visible cleavage, and they were brighter than their usual dark green. "I... It is for the best if I stay on the couch." He rose from the bed and hurried into the bathroom without meeting her gaze.

She had to bite her lip not to laugh out loud. It didn't take much to get him going, and she was going to use that to her advantage.

After peeling off all her clothes except her panties, she got under the covers and waited. So much had happened in the last week it was enough to blow her mind. Julianne had met and mated a fantastic man who was clearly head over heels in love with her, and she was equally in love with him. Sabrina couldn't be happier for her friend. Julianne deserved to be happy, particularly after what she had been through with Steven.

And only a few days after Julianne and Duncan had first met, Duncan introduced them to Leith. There had been an instant attraction between Leith and her, but Sabrina had been determined to keep him at a distance and ignore the attraction as best she could. Little did she know that no more than two days later, they would end up in bed together without him being hurt. In fact, instead of pain, what she'd given him was orgasms by magic. Who knew that was even possible?

The bathroom door opened, and Leith stepped out, wearing nothing but his boxers. He took one look at her in the bed and turned to go into the living room.

"You're not even going to give me a goodnight kiss?" Her voice was intentionally timid and hurt, or at least she hoped it was. She didn't have any experience trying to sound that way.

It did the trick, though. Leith's body tensed, and he turned to her with concern in his gaze. "Yes, I just…" His words died like he didn't know what to say. Then, he moved toward the bed.

Sabrina pushed the covers down and sat up, showing off her naked breasts in the process. Leith's gaze, which had been focused on her face, dropped to her boobs, and he groaned like he was fighting his own reaction to her. But from what she could see, he was losing the fight. The color of his eyes was starting to glow emerald, and when she dropped her gaze to his groin, there was no doubt his cock was reacting to her nakedness.

"You're supposed to sleep, my angel." His voice was rougher than normal.

She got to her feet on the bed, which made her taller than him and placed her breasts almost at a level with his eyes. "I finally have a man that I can give my body to without the risk of hurting him. Can you blame a woman for wanting to explore that?"

His eyes snapped to hers at the same time he reached out and pulled her into his arms. Crushing her against him, he murmured against her breast. "My sweet angel." His lips closed around her left nipple, and he sucked it into his mouth.

Sabrina gasped at the powerful sensation. Tendrils

of pleasure snaked through her body, making her squirm against him. But she wasn't able to move much in his tight embrace.

His tongue flicked against her nipple, and the sensation shot directly to her clit, making it feel like his tongue was tapping against the small bundle of nerves between her legs.

"Leith." She moaned his name and buried her fingers in his long, silky hair as her channel clenched with the need to be filled. She wanted his cock inside her, pushing into her and quenching her need for him.

While holding her tightly with one arm wrapped around her, he let his other hand glide down her spine until it reached her panties. But instead of moving to cup her ass through her panties as she had expected, his hand disappeared down into the small garment. Slowly, his hand slid over her ass and continued underneath until he reached the wet folds of her pussy.

A finger breached her entrance and pushed into her aching channel, and she let out a strange mewling sound that she was sure she had never made before in her life. He pumped his digit into her a few times, and it felt so good, but it wasn't enough.

"I want you inside me." She breathed the words against his forehead, and a shiver raced through his body.

He released her nipple and tipped his head back to meet her gaze. While watching her, he pumped his finger inside her a few more times. His eyes were glowing like the most precious emeralds. "I will get a condom."

"Good." Rocking her hips against his hand, Sabrina bent and crushed her lips to his in a needy kiss. She wanted him more than she had before. A slow burning fire seemed to have started inside her, and she needed it to be stoked into a roaring blaze. Her body wasn't going to get any rest until her climax had burned through her and satisfied this insistent need.

Ripping her mouth away from his, she stared down into his eyes. "Get that condom. I need you."

Leith let her go so quickly she staggered and almost fell off the bed. It seemed she wasn't the only one who was desperate at the moment.

He was back within a few seconds with a small packet in his hand. After getting rid of his boxers, he ripped the packet open and started rolling the condom down his thick, straining shaft. "Take off your panties." Leith's eyes were on her pussy, which was still covered by the lacy fabric.

She quickly stepped out of her panties and stared at him with anticipation. Wetness seeped out of her aching channel and started running down the inside of her thighs. She had never been this turned on in her life. All she could think of was having him thrust his big cock inside her, and if he didn't hurry, she was going to jump him and make it happen.

He closed the distance between them and put a hand between her legs. Two fingers penetrated her and thrusted deep, and she gave a startled cry at the pleasure that surged through her. Her internal muscles clamped down around his digits like they wanted to make sure his fingers stayed in her body, and she rocked against his hand. He slowly pulled his fingers from her body and slid them over her aching clit, making her shudder and moan.

"Leith. No more stalling. I want this inside me."

She bent and wrapped her hand around his cock, before pulling him toward her.

He yelped, and his eyes seemed to lose focus for a second. Then, he grabbed her thighs and lifted her off the bed like she weighed no more than a feather.

She wrapped her legs around his waist as he nudged her entrance with the head of his shaft. She'd never had sex with anyone nearly as well-endowed as Leith, but for some reason, it didn't concern her. If she was his mate, there was no way he was going to be too big for her. He would fit, but it would be tight.

Leith growled as he pushed the crown of his cock inside her, and she felt her eyes go wide at the sensation. Tight was an understatement. He was stretching her to her absolute limit, but it didn't hurt; it felt amazing.

Her channel clenched hard, probably in panic over being invaded by a monster dick, and Leith's eyes rounded. He looked like he didn't know what to do next, but he was too stunned to say anything.

Tilting her pelvis, she forced him deeper into her, and it seemed to snap Leith out of his shock. "You are so tight." His voice was deep and rough, like he hadn't used it in days. "I hope I can last more than half a minute inside you, but if I cannot, I will make it up to you."

He pulled out a little before pushing deeper, and Sabrina felt her jaw slacken. A deep pleasure purred inside her, and fire sparked through her veins. This wasn't going to be like the other orgasms he'd given her. This was going to be deeper and more all-consuming.

After pulling out until only the head of his cock was

still inside her, he thrust hard, seating himself all the way to the hilt. He shuddered and put his forehead on her shoulder. "Please do not move. I need a minute." His breathing was choppy, and his whole body was rigid with tension.

Sabrina had her arms around his neck and was clinging to him for dear life. Her body was screaming at her to move, but she kept still to allow Leith a chance to gain control. She had no trouble understanding his predicament. Just having his long, thick rod so deep inside her was enough to almost push her over the edge. He was filling her so completely that every nerve ending inside her was fully engaged, and even without moving, that was enough to keep her teetering on the brink of ecstasy.

He lifted his head from her shoulder and met her gaze. His eyes were pulsing and sparkling with his desire, and his face was covered with a thin sheen of sweat. "We need to get on the bed. I will not be able to stand through this, and I do not want to hurt you when I go down."

She nodded. "Okay. How—" Her voice broke off when he put a knee on the bed. She had been about to ask him how he wanted to do it, but apparently, he already had a plan.

Without pulling out of her, he slowly moved onto the bed before carefully laying her down on her back. Supporting his upper body on his elbows, he stared down into her eyes. "Are you ready?"

"Yes." She nodded and put her hands on his shoulders. "You feel so good inside me I'm already close. Fuck me, Leith."

He gave her a strained smile, then slowly pulled out

before thrusting deep. A pulse of pleasure ran through her, making her gasp and shiver, and she rocked her hips to encourage Leith to keep moving. Heat was coiling tightly inside her, and her orgasm felt just out of reach.

Another thrust had her mewling and pushing her hips against him in desperation. Leith's jaw was tense, and a deep frown marred his face, probably due to him trying to hold off his own release.

Pulling out slowly, he took a deep breath. But this time when he pushed into her, she deliberately tightened her internal muscles. Leith's eyes went wide for a second before they lost focus. He tipped his head back and roared, and his whole body tensed as he started coming inside her.

Sabrina held her breath as his cock jumped like a wild thing. He was already squeezed so tightly inside her that it was a wonder he was able to move at all. But it was enough to send her soaring. Extreme pleasure pounded through her, and all she could do was hold on through the ecstasy that rocked her body.

Leith roared again, and his whole body shuddered. His cock jerked and strained against her muscles that were holding it in a crushing grip inside her, and she gasped as pleasure flared through her before slowly dying away.

All the tension seemed to leave Leith's body, like he was completely and utterly spent, and the weight of his body came down on top of her and pinned her to the bed.

A weak smile tugged at her lips, and she just reveled in the moment. If someone asked her to describe what had just happened between them, she wasn't sure she could. No words could describe what they had just experienced together. Having an orgasm while in someone's arms was a new experience for her, but even with her limited experience, she was quite sure the ecstasy they had just shared was beyond normal sex. It had to be, or people would stay in bed all the time.

Letting her hands caress Leith's back, she nuzzled her cheek against the side of his head. "Have you passed out from pleasure, or are you still with me?" She turned her head and used her teeth to gently tug on his earlobe.

"I am still here, but it was a close call." His words were muffled against the sheets. "I usually recover pretty fast, but I have never experienced two orgasms back-to-back before. That was a first."

Sabrina smiled. That was what she had thought had happened, and he had just confirmed it.

He lifted his head and met her gaze. "I am sorry I could not hold on. I should have waited until you had your pleasure before I came, but I can give you another orgasm with my mouth to make it up to you. I do not think my dick can take any more action for a little while."

Chuckling, she put her hands on his cheeks. "What you just gave me was amazing, and we're going to repeat it soon, but not tonight. I'm exhausted, and we have an important day tomorrow. Let's go to bed, my love. I want to sleep in your arms."

"My love." A big grin spread across his face. "You called me *my love*." His lips crushed against hers in a hard kiss before he pulled back. He looked so happy that Sabrina had to laugh.

"I need to get rid of this condom." He brushed a quick kiss against her tingling lips. "Will you join me in the shower? I am sweaty and sticky all over."

Smiling, she slowly shook her head. "That's not a good idea. Seeing your fantastic body dripping wet will be too much for my sanity right now. And it will definitely not help me sleep."

He grinned. "So naked and dripping wet is a turn-on then?"

"Absolutely." She grinned back at him.

"Good to know. I will save that information for when I need it." His eyes were glittering with amusement. Then, he was suddenly up and moving toward the bathroom. "I will be quick."

Sweaty and sticky, indeed. She was, too, and she'd have a quick shower after he was done. It was true what she'd said about seeing him wet, and they needed sleep to be able to handle whatever Ambrosia would throw at them the next day. If they managed to find her.

CHAPTER 17

Leith woke when the alarm on his phone went off. He had slept like a baby, even though he'd had his hot female in his arms all night. But after the two mind-blowing orgasms she'd given him, it wasn't a surprise. Unfortunately, his body seemed to have forgotten that already. His dick was as hard as rock and throbbing with the need to claim his mate, but he had no intention of succumbing to his desire. They had to get up and go meet Duncan, Julianne, and Callum for breakfast.

"Good morning." Sabrina lifted her head from where it had been resting on his chest. She looked tired, and he felt himself frowning. "Don't worry, I'm not that tired." A smile curved her beautiful, sinfully hot mouth.

Staring at her lips, he found himself remembering how she'd looked with those lips stretched around his cock while she took all of him. It was the most erotic sight he'd ever seen in his life, and he already looked forward to the next time she would do that to him. But it wasn't going to be this morning.

He cleared his throat and raised his gaze to hers. But before he could say anything, her hand closed around his shaft and gave it a tug. "Sabrina." His voice broke, and he cleared his throat again, only to groan when she reached down and fondled his balls.

"I want to make you come before we go to breakfast." She lowered her head and licked his nipple before tugging on it with her teeth. He jerked as a mixture of pleasure and pain shot directly to his hard length, making it throb more insistently.

"Sabrina." He yelled her name and reached down to remove her hand from his balls, but instead she grabbed his cock and gave it a firm tug.

"Don't you want me to give you an orgasm?" She flicked her tongue over the nipple she had just bitten. "I think you need it. It might be a while before we get back to the hotel."

She had a point, but he was reluctant to give in to her. They would be late for breakfast with the others. Then again being late wasn't a crime, and he owed it to his mate to let her do what she wanted with him. She was the most important person in his life. "Only if I can do something for you as well."

"Okay." She sat up and flung the sheets off them. "I'll do you first." She moved to settle between his legs, but he stopped her.

"Or." He reached between her legs and gently skimmed her folds. "We can try doing each other at the same time. Do you think that will work?"

Heat flared in her eyes while she considered his words. "You mean I'll sit on your face while I suck your dick?"

"Yes. Will you still manage to swallow my cock while you are sitting like that?" A shiver ran through his body at the thought. He wanted to pleasure her while she deep-throated him. He wouldn't last long, but it would be fantastic, and he was going to make sure it was for her as well.

"I think so." She nodded. "I've never tried it before, but it should be fine."

"Just stop if it is uncomfortable in any way, okay?" He studied her face.

"Of course." Sabrina smiled.

Without any preamble he yanked her into his arms and kissed her hard. His mate might seem cold to some people, and she had tried that with him as well in the beginning, but it was all a façade to keep people at a distance. Her fear had demanded that she didn't allow people too close, and with humans that had been a correct decision. But with him those precautions weren't necessary, and it allowed her to show her passionate side.

He cupped the back of her head with one hand as he plundered her sweet mouth with his tongue. With his other hand he found her breast and rolled her nipple between his thumb and index finger. She moaned into his mouth, and he wished they had time to take it slow and play. But they didn't. The others would be waiting soon, and he was getting too desperate to wait much longer. His shaft was so hard it was getting uncomfortable, evidence that his need to claim her was increasing.

He broke their kiss and pulled away to stare into her eyes. "You are the most amazing woman I have ever met. I am decidedly the luckiest man alive."

Sabrina laughed. "Some of your friends seem to think the same thing with their mates."

He grinned. "I am the luckiest. There is no denying that fact. But it is probably best not to crush their illusion that they are. No point destroying their happiness now is there?"

Laughing, she shook her head at him. "Whatever you say, my love."

"Now let us start. I want your juicy pussy in my face." He kept his eyes on her face as he lay back on the bed. A blush reddened her cheeks, and she quickly turned her head away from him. It was intriguing how she seemed comfortable with their activities in bed and wasn't reluctant to take charge, yet she blushed like she was inexperienced or shy.

She moved around and placed her knees next to his shoulders. He gripped her thighs and guided her into position.

He was just opening his mouth to get started when she wrapped her hand around his cock. His whole body jerked, and he pushed his tongue into her tight sheath a bit more forcefully than he had intended.

Sabrina squealed and squeezed his shaft in her hand. He almost came off the bed at the feeling and forced his tongue as far as he could inside her. She moaned just before she wrapped her lips around the head of his dick, forcing a growl from him.

Sabrina shivered and moaned as she took more of him into her mouth, and he groaned and vibrated his tongue inside her channel. What she was doing to him was quickly removing his ability to think. If he was going to be able to make her come before he did, he had to try to distance himself from what she was doing to him and concentrate on what he wanted to do to her. A near impossible task, but he wanted to hear her screams of pleasure and feel her body rock in ecstasy. And he had to be quick, because he wasn't going to last long.

He pulled his tongue out of her body and put his lips around her pleasure button. It was already swollen with her need, and he sucked it into his mouth. She shuddered against him right before she swallowed his cock. He felt his eyes widen and his fingers dig into her thighs at the amazing feeling, but he focused on her sensitive flesh in his mouth.

He flicked his tongue against her clit while sucking on it, and his eyes almost bugged out of his head when she moaned with his cock in her throat. It brought him right to the edge, forcing him to reconsider his actions.

He moved his arm across both her thighs to lock her in place before maneuvering his other arm into position. It was a little awkward, and he had to tip his head back a little to be able to do it, but he managed to squeeze his hand between her channel and his face without letting go of her clit.

While vibrating his tongue against her swollen nub, he drove two fingers deep inside her tight channel. She jerked and tried to move away, but he just increased the vibration of his tongue while pumping his fingers inside her.

It didn't take long before her muscles clamped down on his fingers when she started coming. Her body shuddered, and she moaned around his cock, and he couldn't hold on anymore. Pleasure detonated and rushed through his body just as Sabrina's magic blasted through him, igniting every cell in his body. His cock jerked and jetted his seed down her throat, and he heard himself roar like a wild beast. His release pulsed through him for what seemed like a long time before it slowly let him go, leaving him to breathe like he had just run a marathon in fifteen minutes uphill.

Sabrina was on her side beside him with her head on his thigh, and she was breathing as hard as he was. His body was spent, and it would have been wonderful to be able to go back to sleep for a while, but the sight of his beautiful mate made him smile and gave him new energy.

He lifted her head off his thigh and moved around until he was propped on his elbow beside her. Using his index finger, he pushed a stray lock of hair behind her ear. She had just given him one hell of a blowjob, yet her appearance was near flawless. It didn't even seem like she made an effort to make it so. She'd looked a little tired as she woke this morning but that was as imperfect as he had ever seen her, which was saying something. She just didn't seem to have it in her to be less than perfect.

She cracked an eyelid and looked at him. "I could use a couple of hours of sleep now. That tongue of yours is lethal."

He laughed. "I could say the same thing about your mouth and your magic."

"In that order?" She lifted her head and raised an eyebrow at him.

He chuckled. "Yes. I would take your mouth over your magic every time."

"Good to know." She smiled and sat up. "But I think we need to get going."

"We do, my angel." Unfortunately. He was already regretting that fact.

CHAPTER 18

The first person they saw when they walked into the breakfast restaurant was Julianne, and her face split into a smile as soon as she saw them. Julianne hurried over and gave Sabrina such a big hug she had to take a step back not to fall over.

"Julianne, it seems you've missed me. I guess it wasn't as much fun traveling with Duncan as it was with me." Sabrina couldn't help herself, and of course, it was better to get the first shot because she knew what was coming. Julianne was bound to tease her about giving in to her attraction to Leith, with a couple of *What did I tell you* remarks included in the speech at strategic places.

Her friend laughed and stepped back. "Are you trying to make me forget the fact that you're almost half an hour late for breakfast? If so, it's not working." Julianne's eyes were sparkling with amusement. "I really hope it was something fun that made you late."

Sabrina didn't want to answer that, but Julianne

obviously didn't expect her to either. Her friend turned around and headed toward a table in the corner where Duncan and Callum were sitting.

Leith clasped Sabrina's hand in his while they walked over. He smiled down at her when she met his eyes.

"About time you decided to join us." Duncan's eyes were filled with amusement. "Julianne has been hovering by the door since we arrived. And we arrived early. It's been nice having breakfast with Callum, but I had hoped to have my woman by my side as well."

Sabrina smiled. "She's been waiting to tease me for days. I guess she was anxious to get started."

Leith squeezed her hand before letting it go. "Then, I guess we need to give her something to tease you about."

She turned to look at him. "What do you—"

Her question was cut off when his mouth covered hers. His arms wrapped around her, and he bent her backward as he plundered her mouth in front of the entire restaurant. She could hear people laughing and cheering them on, but she didn't care as she kissed him back. He was hers, and the whole world might as well know it.

He broke their kiss slowly before straightening and staring at her with the corner of his mouth lifted slightly in resemblance of a smile. "Are you hungry, my angel?"

Sabrina wasn't sure what he was asking. Was he talking about food or something else? She obviously took too long to answer, or perhaps it was her dazed expression from his kiss.

"Food, Sabrina." There was amusement in Leith's

eyes.

The whole table erupted in laughter, and she felt her cheeks heat. The joke was on her, but she found she didn't mind. These people were truly happy for them. But it didn't mean she was going to leave it like that. She made sure her expression was neutral before she spoke. "I've already eaten, but I'm sure some food would be nice as well. How about you?"

Leith's jaw dropped, and his eyes brightened ever so slightly. Julianne gasped, and the guys at the table roared with laughter.

Sabrina smiled sweetly at Leith. "What's the matter? Don't you want anything more to eat? Something juicy perhaps?"

Snapping his mouth shut, he narrowed his eyes at her. "I am thinking of ways to stop that mouth of yours, and a number of activities comes to mind. We will be trying some of those later."

She laughed and rose onto her toes to plant a quick kiss on his lips. Then, she took his hand and tugged on it. "Come, my love. Let's check out the breakfast buffet."

They filled their plates before returning to the others. Sabrina hadn't realized how hungry she was until she saw all the delicious food, and she heaped her plate with more food than she could possibly eat on her own. Hopefully, she could put some of it on Leith's plate. She didn't like wasting food.

It was strange how close she felt to the man already. Even considering asking him to eat some of the food on her plate was something she had never done before with anyone. She'd never been in a relationship like that. Of course, that was a choice she'd made herself, a choice she'd had to make, but still. In just three days she had grown more attached to this man than she would have thought possible in a month. They still didn't know each other that well, but for some reason, it didn't matter. She felt comfortable and safe around him.

"So you have obviously gotten better acquainted in the last couple of days." Julianne's statement pulled Sabrina out of her own head.

Turning to look at her friend, Sabrina smiled. "That's a fair observation."

Julianne smiled. "I am so happy for you, the both of you. I really hoped you would give in to the attraction between you. It was what everyone hoped."

"Everyone?" Sabrina knew Julianne had seen her attraction to Leith, but she hadn't realized that all the others had figured it out as well. She had clearly been less subtle than she thought. Not that it mattered.

Julianne nodded. "Yes, everyone. You couldn't keep your eyes away from each other for more than a few seconds at a time."

Sabrina smiled. "Well, it's all out in the open now."

"Well and truly I'd say." Julianne lifted an eyebrow at her, clearly referring to Sabrina's rather crude words earlier. "I thought Leith was going to grab you and carry you right back to your room."

Chuckling, Sabrina shook her head before turning to look at her soon-to-be mate. Leith was deep in a serious discussion with Duncan and Callum about Ambrosia.

"I'm sorry, can you repeat that, Callum?" Sabrina smiled when he turned to look at her.

"Certainly." Callum's brown eyes were warm when

he smiled. "Ambrosia's phone was on this morning for about an hour. The movement indicated that she was driving around Inverness, stopping here and there for a few minutes at a time. I haven't been able to figure out why. The locations seemed to be random, and no shops were open at that time. And most of the time, it didn't even seem like she left the car. My best guess is that she was looking for someone or something."

"But her phone is turned off again now?" Leith was frowning.

Callum nodded. "Yes, it has been since seven thirty this morning. I would've been notified if she turned it back on." He patted his breast pocket that was holding his phone.

"Do you know where she's been staying since she arrived in Inverness?" Sabrina asked.

"Unfortunately, no." Callum sighed. "She only turns her phone on for an hour or two a day, and she keeps it turned off at night. It's strange. I mean nobody does that. People keep their phones on all the time, unless the battery dies, or they want to hide where they are. She seems to be in the latter category, which makes me suspect we're not the only ones looking for her."

"Shit." Duncan stared at Callum. "It never even crossed my mind. Which name is the phone registered to?"

Callum chuckled, but there was no amusement in his eyes. "Jane Smith, and no I don't believe that's her real name. Her address is a P-O box in Edinburgh, which is also registered to Jane Smith. No forwarding address that I can find. She knows how to hide, that's for sure."

"Phone register?" Leith picked up his cup and took a sip of his coffee.

Callum nodded. "She's only had the phone number for six months, and in that time, she's called exactly two people, Jack the alpha panther and her daughter Mary. I haven't had time to delve into Mary's records yet but I will. If Mary really is Ambrosia's daughter, I might be able to establish Ambrosia's true identity via Mary."

Julianne sighed. "Seems like we can do nothing but wait until she turns her phone back on." She cocked her head. "Would you be able to check cameras in the area she was driving around this morning?"

"Yes." Callum smiled. "I checked a couple of them before I came down to meet you for breakfast, but there wasn't much to see other than the car she was driving. I've got the license plate number, and it's a rental as expected, registered to a..." He left the sentence hanging.

"Jane Smith. Fuck." Duncan frowned. "So she has a full fake persona set up with driver's license, phone, and God knows what else. Would she do all that just to get her revenge on shifters, or was she already planning something sinister, and her daughter's death just altered her plans somewhat? I don't like this. She might be more dangerous than we thought."

Leith nodded with a considering expression on his face. "Possibly, or she already knew about shifters and the fact that they tend to be wealthy and well-connected. She might have realized early on that the only way to live long enough to have her revenge was to be able to hide. It would be easy to track her otherwise, and I am sure she has already figured out that many shifters will not hesitate to kill her for what she is trying to do."

Callum nodded. "Good point. But it takes connections and money to be able to create a fake persona like she has. Someone knows her real identity, and possibly her intentions. That someone might even be backing her for all we know."

Sabrina frowned. "If that's the case, this is much bigger than one woman wanting to get revenge for her daughter. I sincerely hope that's not the case, because if it is then this won't end even if we stop Ambrosia. Her sponsor will just get someone else to finish the job, whatever that job really is. I'm not sure we know the end goal yet, and it's hard to stop something when you don't know the objective."

Julianne visibly shuddered. "I really hope this is just about her daughter. Not that her daughter's death isn't tragic or significant, but I don't like to think that this is part of some larger scheme aimed to hurt shifters. Isn't there some kind of supernatural police that could handle this?"

Callum laughed and shook his head, but the other guys didn't join in. A meaningful look passed between Leith and Duncan, and Sabrina narrowed her eyes at her mate. Leith and Duncan knew something that Callum didn't, which struck her as odd. Perhaps it had something to do with Callum being so much younger than the other two. According to Leith, Callum was in his early thirties, which was considered barely adult among shifters. And the fact that he was running some kind of security company might not be enough to qualify him to know classified information in the supernatural world.

Leith leaned in and spoke softly close to her ear. "Are you not hungry, my angel? You have hardly touched your food."

Sabrina looked down at her plate. There was still some food left, but she had actually eaten quite a lot. "I took too much. Everything looked so good, and I was hungry. It's the reason I try to avoid going grocery shopping when I'm hungry, because I'll always end up buying far more than I need." She lifted her gaze to his. "It looks bad leaving all this food, though. Would you like some of it? I haven't touched the food I haven't eaten."

He shook his head, but the corner of his lips lifted into a small smile. "I think I have had enough, but if you feel bad we can switch plates so it appears I am the one who did not finish my food."

Smiling, Sabrina shook her head. "No, it doesn't matter. I'm sure I'm not the only one here to leave food on her plate. Thank you for offering, though."

Leith gave a single nod. "As you wish. Are you ready to go?"

She nodded.

"Why don't we gather in our suite upstairs?" Leith swung his gaze around the table. "We still need to plan how to approach Ambrosia."

"Sounds good." Callum nodded and rose from the table. "I'll just go grab my laptop, and I'll be right there. Which floor is it?"

"Third floor." Leith rose as well. "To the left at the end of the corridor. By the back stairs."

Leith reached out his hand for her, and Sabrina grabbed it as she got up from the table.

Duncan and Julianne stood, and Duncan put his

arm around his mate's shoulders. "We'll be there in a few minutes."

"Good." Leith gave them a short nod before turning to Sabrina and tugging gently on her hand.

They walked out of the restaurant before Leith steered her toward the lift. She was a bit surprised. They had taken the stairs while staying at the hotel. Never once had he wanted to take the lift. But she didn't question him about it. He probably wanted to get to the room quickly to make sure it was tidy before the others arrived.

As soon as they stepped inside the lift and the doors closed, Leith pushed her against the wall and captured her lips in a hard kiss. It only lasted a few seconds before he pulled away to stare into her eyes with eyes that were brightening into emerald. "I want you." His voice was deeper than normal. "Fuck, I want you. I have been fighting to stay in control ever since you said you had already eaten."

Something hard was poking into her stomach, and she kept her eyes on his while she reached between them and palmed his cock through his jeans. "I think you're losing that fight, and we don't have time to take care of this now. You invited guests over remember?" Which was frustrating, because she would have loved to rip his clothes off and ride him until they both came screaming.

He groaned and squeezed his eyes shut for a second before opening them. "We can tell them to give us half an hour. They'll understand."

The doors opened on the third floor, and Leith grabbed her hand and pulled her out into the corridor. Thankfully, there was nobody around, and they walked quickly to their suite.

Leith closed the door behind them and pulled her into the bedroom. When he turned to her, his eyes were sparkling like jewels in the sun, and his jaw was tense with raw need. But there was a look of indecision on his face, and he made no move to pull her close.

"Leith?" She cocked her head in question as she studied his face. "Do you want to tell the others to give us some time alone before they show up? Or do you want to go ahead with the planning as agreed? You look like you don't know what to do."

He pulled in a deep breath before letting it out slowly. "I think we need the time to plan for when Ambrosia turns on her phone again. It could happen at any time, and we need to be prepared. As much as I need you right now, it is not an optimal use of our time."

Sabrina nodded slowly. He was right, even though she had hoped he would choose to postpone the others' visit. She felt hot, and her girl parts were screaming for attention. He wasn't the only one who was aching with need at the moment. "I'm sorry I can't let you claim me with so many people close by. I know our need to mate is making us more amorous than usual. But I can't take the chance that someone gets hurt, and that includes you."

"Our need." He studied her face. "You are feeling it too." A small smile tugged at his lips. "That is a comfort, even if it is a small one."

She chuckled. "Yeah, better to be fucked together. Or in our case, not fucked together."

"Exactly." He grinned and took a step closer, like he intended to pull her into his arms. But then he frowned and backed away a couple of steps. "I cannot touch you right now. I would not be able to stop, and the others will arrive any minute."

As if on cue, there was a knock on the door.

Sabrina smiled. "I can get that. Why don't you take a minute and come out when you're ready, okay?"

Leith nodded. "Thank you."

She walked out of the bedroom and closed the door behind her before heading toward the entrance to the suite. Callum smiled at her when she opened the door.

"Come in, Callum."

"Wait for us." Julianne's voice sounded from down the corridor.

Sabrina opened the door wide and welcomed them all into the suite and indicated the couch. "Take a seat. Leith will be out in a second."

Duncan, Julianne, and Callum sat down on the couch, and Sabrina pulled up a chair and sat down across the low table from them.

"I've been thinking about Ambrosia's abilities and how little we actually know about her witch powers." Sabrina swung her gaze between the people on the couch. "Witches can have different abilities and be more or less powerful, but we don't know a lot about what Ambrosia can do apart from what Steph told us."

Julianne pursed her lips in thought. "Taking control of someone's mind or will seems like a major power, though, and a useful one in a fight. And from what Steph said, the evil bitch seemed to be able to do that quite easily."

Nodding, Sabrina frowned. "Yes, and she even healed Steph while she kept her control over Jack.

Being able to use two abilities at the same time is not common for witches as far as I know. Most witches can only focus on one thing at a time."

"I don't like the sound of that." Leith's voice from behind her made Sabrina turn to meet his gaze. "Perhaps we should wait on confronting Ambrosia until Steph can join us." Leith swung his gaze to Duncan. "Have you talked to Trevor?"

Duncan nodded. "Yes. They're going to visit a panther clan at noon. They'll head this way after that."

"Good." Leith walked up to Sabrina and put his hands on her shoulders. "I would feel better with Steph supporting you, my angel. She might not know her abilities well yet, but she is powerful."

Duncan put his arm around Julianne and pulled her tighter against him, like he felt the need to protect her. "I don't know how much he can do against Ambrosia, but Trevor's alpha power is formidable. Other than you, Leith, I don't know any shifter who's as powerful as Trevor. Having him with us as well might be useful."

"I agree." Callum had opened his laptop and was staring at the screen. "It's impossible to say when Ambrosia will turn her phone back on. And where. Not to be negative, but for all we know the next time she turns it on, she'll be in Edinburgh or London. Hopefully, that won't be the case. But it's like Sabrina said earlier, it all depends on her objective."

Leith's phone rang, and he pulled it out of his pocket and took a look at the screen before answering. "Henry, how are you doing this morning?"

Sabrina tried to hear what Henry was saying, but it was too low for her to hear.

Leith narrowed his eyes. "Just now? Is she still there? Wait, I will put you on speaker." He pulled the phone from his ear and touched the screen before putting the phone on the low table. "I am here with Sabrina, Duncan and his mate, Julianne, and Callum, a young wolf who's a friend of Duncan's. Please tell them what you just told me."

Henry's voice sounded over the phone. "Ambrosia was here around fifteen minutes ago, and she may still be in the area. Vamika saw her in the drive but when she approached the witch, something happened, and Vamika can't remember the next few minutes."

Sabrina met Julianne's gaze. "Sounds like Ambrosia has been practicing her mind control again. It's one of her known abilities."

"Mind control?" Henry didn't sound pleased. "Can she do that to anyone? And more importantly, can she make you forget that she has subjected you to it or even that you have met her at all?"

"We don't know." But Sabrina suspected that Ambrosia could make people forget that she had controlled them. Steph had mentioned that Ambrosia had controlled Jack, but he had still seemed to trust the evil witch afterward. It didn't seem logical that someone like Jack would trust a person whom he knew had manipulated him.

"Fuck!" Henry was obviously angry and with good reason.

"We can head in your direction now, Henry." Leith swung his gaze around the table to look at each one of them, and they all nodded their agreement. "It might be a good idea to gather everyone in your pack in one place. We know she can manipulate one person at a time, but there is no reason to believe that she can control several people at once. You are safer together than alone. We will be there as soon as we can. If you see her again, please notify me."

"Thank you, Leith." Henry sighed. "We'll talk when you get here."

They said goodbye, and Leith ended the call. "Well, now we know where Ambrosia is, or at least where she was a few minutes ago."

Callum nodded. "I'm setting up a continuous scan using the feed from a couple of cameras on the main road between Henry's pack and Inverness, just in case she heads back that way. The program will notify me as soon as her license plate is identified, and then we'll know that she's on her way back to Inverness. I can set up the same system for other cameras on roads heading in other directions, but I need to identify which cameras to use first so it will take more time."

"Thank you, Callum." Duncan smiled at his friend. "There's more than one person in this room who can work magic, apparently."

Callum shook his head like he didn't agree or perhaps felt a bit uncomfortable with the praise, but there was a small smile on his face. "Nah, it's not that difficult. You just need the right software, that's all."

Julianne laughed. "After you've hacked into the camera systems, you mean."

"What kind of wolf do you think I am?" Callum feigned a shocked expression. Then he grinned. "The hacking takes some experience; I'll give you that. But the two cameras I'm using now are live on the open web, so no hacking was necessary. That's why I could set it up so quickly."

Leith cleared his throat softly. "I am sorry to break into your explanation, Callum, but I think we should leave immediately."

Callum nodded and closed his laptop. "I agree. No need to apologize. Let's go."

They all rose, and Duncan, Julianne, and Callum left after agreeing to meet them in the hotel garage.

CHAPTER 19

Leith drove fast after they left the city behind. He wasn't sure why Ambrosia was checking out Henry's pack, but there might be a few possible explanations. None of them were positive, though, so there was no doubt that Henry and his wolves needed their support. Whether they would find Ambrosia when they got there was no guarantee, and Leith had reasons to hope they didn't without Steph to support Sabrina, but at least they would talk to Vamika and find out all she could remember of the encounter with the evil witch.

"I wonder if she's looking for Freddie." Sabrina's voice made him glance at her where she was sitting in the passenger seat. "Henry assumes he's dead, but Ambrosia might not think so. Maybe she thinks the pack is protecting him. If that's the case, they might be in real danger."

Leith nodded. "I agree. Or she's trying to find a new susceptible victim to be able to increase her power through a mating bond. Henry will never fall for her promises, but some of the wolves in his pack might. There are still a few who resent him for taking over and changing the rules. The friends of the previous alpha had a lot of advantages that Henry removed as soon as he became the new alpha."

"That's a possibility." Sabrina frowned like she was considering something. "Henry's questions made me think. I do believe Ambrosia can make someone forget that she has manipulated them, and she may even be able to make someone forget meeting her at all. But I'm not so sure she can control someone to such a degree that they will perform anything more than simple tasks under her influence. Based on what Steph and Michael told me, it seems Ambrosia can stop a person's brain from functioning properly, like she can put someone in neutral for a while."

Leith let her words sink in. "So, if I understand you correctly, what you are saying is that Ambrosia cannot manipulate a person to carry out a task, she can only stop them from acting."

Sabrina nodded. "Pretty much. She can tell them to sit or stand or something simple that doesn't really require much conscious awareness, but I don't think she can make them carry out something more complex like fighting someone or leading a conversation. I cannot be sure of this, of course, but it makes sense. If she could manipulate someone to do whatever she wanted, she wouldn't need their agreement and could pick whoever best suited her objectives."

"And that is not what she has done so far, as far as we know." Leith nodded to himself as much as to Sabrina. "She has picked shifters who believe what she tells them and agree with her plan. I think you are right. But how will this help us stop her?"

"I'm not sure that it will, but Henry sounded worried when we mentioned mind control, and knowing that Ambrosia won't be able to make a person into a tool she can wield to do whatever she wants, will reduce his concern somewhat. It doesn't mean she's not dangerous, though."

"That is true." There had been a definite note of concern in Henry's voice, and Leith had no trouble understanding why. "We know that Ambrosia can heal and control people to a certain degree. But are there indications that she has other abilities as well?"

Sabrina glanced at him. "Not that I know of, but I've never met her in person. Meeting her and talking to her might reveal something else, but I'm not sure I would be able to pick it up, anyway. I don't know the full spectrum of witch abilities out there. I don't think anyone does. We don't have a network like shifters do, and we don't seek each other out. The risk is too great of detection by the general public.

"Or…it was. There are quite a few people who pretend to be witches now, and you have the whole cosplay scene. You can get away with a lot these days compared to before, but people a little older than me are still wary of the consequences if you do something out of the ordinary among normal people. People would believe it was some kind of trick, though. They would never believe it was real. And that fact should act as an encouragement to seek out other real witches, but unfortunately, it hasn't yet. Hiding who we are and what we can do is one of the lessons we are taught from birth, and it's hard to go against something that fundamental in our training."

Listening to Sabrina talking about abilities and hiding what you were, he couldn't help thinking about his own promise to tell her what he was when they were mated. They weren't mated yet, but with everything that had happened between them, he wanted to tell her, anyway. But it would have to wait until the next time they had a chance to be alone together. They would arrive at Henry's in just a few minutes, and they needed to be focused when they did. Henry hadn't contacted him again, which probably meant that the pack hadn't encountered Ambrosia again, but they had to be prepared for anything when they got there just in case.

Apprehension stiffened his spine. There weren't many things that scared him, but the thought of his mate being in danger was definitely one of them. "Please promise me that you will be careful, my angel. We may not meet Ambrosia today, but if we do, do not take any chances. Stay close to me, and I will protect you and support you with my power. Do not go off on your own, or I will not be able to help you."

Sabrina turned her head and looked at him with one of her eyebrows raised like she was going to ask him who the fuck he thought he was.

She opened her mouth to say something, but he beat her to it. "I love you, my angel, and the thought of you putting yourself in danger scares me more than anything ever has."

Sabrina's eyes widened in surprise for a second before she snapped her mouth shut with an audible clack and turned to look straight ahead.

"It should not come as a surprise to you that I do not want you putting yourself at risk." He glanced at her profile and her unreadable expression. "Does that anger you?"

A small smile curved her lips. "No, I'm just not used to a man worrying about me and wanting to protect me. And..." She paused like she was considering what to say. "I'm not used to having a man who loves me. And it's not just the fact that you love me that feels unfamiliar, it's the fact that you know who I am. I don't have to pretend with you, because there is no part of me that I need to hide."

The big house they had visited just the day before came into view, and Leith parked the car close to the porch. He turned to Sabrina and cupped the side of her face. Staring into her eyes, he smiled. "It makes me happy that you feel you can be yourself around me." He leaned in and covered her lips with his. He wanted so much more than a kiss, but it was all they had time for.

A knock on the driver's side window interrupted their moment. Pulling away from Sabrina, he smiled at her before turning to see Duncan grinning at them through the window.

***

Callum stared up at the big house. According to Duncan, it was the alpha's home and the main house used for pack activities and meetings. There were other smaller houses spread around the large pack property, but those were occupied by families as well as single pack members.

He had never met Henry or anyone from his pack before. Meeting new shifters was usually an unpleasant experience, and he avoided those when he could, but he had agreed to help Duncan, and he wasn't going to back out of that promise just to avoid some unpleasantness.

"Where is everyone?" Duncan stared up at the house with a frown on his face as Leith and Sabrina stepped out of their car. "It's awfully quiet around here."

"I agree." Leith narrowed his eyes in concern and let his gaze wander around what they could see of the property surrounding the house. "Too quiet."

Leith had barely uttered the last word when there was a sound from inside the house. A big hallway was visible through the open front door, and a tall red-haired man stepped into the hallway from a room toward the back of the house.

The man strode toward them, looking relieved. "There you are. Thank you for coming."

Leith gave a single nod, and his expression smoothed. "No trouble at all, Henry. And thank you for getting in touch so quickly. Have you seen her again?"

"No." Henry shook his head. "But we're all gathered in the house." Using his thumb, he indicated the large house behind him. "She might still be around, even if we haven't seen her. I don't like that she can mess with people's minds. That shit is fucked up."

"Let's go inside, Henry." Duncan nodded toward the house. "I would feel better with my mate inside those walls rather than out here in the open. It might not make much of a difference, but that's how I feel."

"Absolutely." Henry turned around and started walking, obviously expecting them to follow. "We can do introductions inside."

Callum held back and let the others enter the house

in front of him. He followed behind Leith.

Henry led them into a large office and indicated for them to sit down on a big corner sofa at one end of the room. But before he could move over to the couch, Callum felt someone else enter the room behind him.

His spine stiffened, and the small hairs on the back of his neck stood up. He wanted to turn around, but he was afraid to do so. There was something special about the woman who had just entered the room, but he didn't know what it was. He was sure it was a woman, though, even though he hadn't turned around to look at her.

"Vamika, please sit down." Henry looked at the woman behind Callum. "I'm sure everyone would like to hear in your own words what happened when you saw Ambrosia. Or at least what you can remember. But first I think introductions are in order."

Duncan nodded and put his arm around his mate. "This is my beautiful mate, Julianne."

Julianne smiled at Henry before moving her gaze to the woman who was still behind Callum. "Pleased to meet you."

Henry gave her a smile that didn't quite reach his eyes. The man looked worried. "Pleased to meet you, too, Julianne."

"And still standing over there is my friend Callum." Duncan grinned at him.

Callum forced himself to smile at Henry, but it felt more like a grimace than a smile. "Nice to meet you."

Henry gave him a small nod of acknowledgement. "Nice to meet you, too, Callum. Please have a seat."

Callum couldn't refuse the alpha's request to sit

down, but he had to force himself to move. The thought of showing the woman behind him that he was lacking was almost physically painful, but why it should matter so much to him he had no idea. He walked slowly over to the couch to make his limp less noticeable, but there was no hiding the fact that one of his legs was weaker and more unstable than the other.

Sitting down at one end of the couch, he stared at the low table in front of him. The woman who had been standing behind him came over and sat down in an armchair across the table from him, but he resisted the urge to look at her.

Henry sat down on the sofa by the end of the table. "For those of you who haven't met her already, this is Vamika. She is the one who encountered Ambrosia earlier today."

Callum lifted his gaze to look at the woman who was having such a strange effect on him, and he was stunned when he met her dark-brown gaze. She was staring at him with what could only be described as open hostility, and to say he was taken aback was putting it mildly. A stab of pain in his chest made him wince, and he tore his gaze away from hers. He had no idea why she was looking at him like that since he'd never met her before. She didn't know anything about him, but it was obvious she didn't like him. And the only reasonable explanation was that it was due to his disability.

It was nothing new that some shifters treated him like he was lesser because of his disability, but they were usually more subtle about it when surrounded by people who were his friends. He was seldom invited to celebrations or to run with other shifters in animal form, even though his wolf form showed less of a disability than his human one. His wolf had a slight weakness in his right hindleg, but it wasn't pronounced, and he could run as fast as some of the other males he knew. But that didn't seem to make any difference to them. He was still the shifter with a physical disability, something that was practically unheard of among his kind.

Henry was saying something, but Callum's mind was a mess of thoughts and emotions, and he was struggling to focus on what was being said. A smooth, low voice snagged his attention, though, and before he could stop himself, he lifted his gaze to stare at Vamika.

She wasn't looking at him, but her expression spoke of a simmering anger. "I was just coming out of the house when I noticed Ambrosia walking up the drive. She was still a hundred yards from the house, but she stopped when she saw me, like she hadn't intended to make her presence known. I walked off the porch and approached her, but before I could reach her, her eyes brightened, and the next I remember I am standing in the drive alone. Everything between is a blank, like I skipped time. I know I didn't lose more than three minutes, but I have no idea what happened in that time. Ambrosia was nowhere to be seen when I woke from whatever she did to me, and I don't know whether she left the property or hid somewhere. Nobody else has seen her, or at least nobody remembers seeing her."

Callum had been staring at her while she was talking. She was easily the most beautiful woman he had ever seen. Dark flawless complexion, big dark-brown eyes framed by thick black lashes, and that hair. His hands were itching to play with her long, shiny black hair. It was currently controlled in a thick braid that was hanging over one shoulder and breast and reaching down to her hip. And he had to curb an almost uncontrollable urge to loosen her braid and let his hands run through her long tresses. He had a thing for long hair, and hers was amazing.

Her eyes were suddenly on him again, and he felt himself pull back from her like he could get farther away by pushing himself into the seatback of the couch. The anger wasn't as evident this time, but it was still there. Instead of looking away, though, he held her gaze and even tried to relax his expression into a smile. His apprehension still had a firm grip on his spine, making his whole body tense, but he wanted to give a good impression, even if she didn't like him.

"I would like to take a walk around the property just to check if I can feel Ambrosia's power." Sabrina speaking caused Vamika to turn toward her. "It might be for nothing if she's no longer here, but I'd like to try, anyway. Would you mind coming with me, Vamika?"

Vamika nodded slowly. "I can do that, although I doubt she's still here."

Sabrina frowned. "Why do you say that?"

Vamika shrugged. "I don't know. Just a feeling I've got."

"Can all witches control people like Ambrosia can?" Henry's expression was one of concern. "I've never heard of anyone able to do something like that before. To be honest it was a bit of a shock when Vamika told me what happened to her."

"I understand that." Sabrina smiled. "But as far as I know, it's not a common witch ability. I believe it takes more power than most witches have. And based on what we know of Ambrosia so far, what she's doing is not so much controlling someone as stopping someone. I doubt she can actually make a person do anything other than obeying simple commands like sit or stand."

"Are you sure?" Henry looked doubtful.

Sabrina shook her head. "If you're asking me whether I can swear that's how it is, then no. But I strongly believe Ambrosia is unable to make someone carry out a complex task that requires more concentration than walking on even ground."

Nodding, Henry pulled in a deep breath before letting it out slowly. "I guess that's better than what I thought before. Having someone running around able to manipulate anyone into doing anything wasn't a good prospect, and I must admit that I was planning to take her down without warning if I happened to see her. Better safe than sorry you know."

"I understand that." Leith put his arm around Sabrina's shoulders and pulled her close. "But I for one am still prepared to eliminate her when I see her. She might be grieving her daughter, but to take her revenge on shifters in general is unacceptable. The only reasons she has not caused severe damage already are sheer luck and the fact that she picked the wrong people to mess with. If we do not stop her soon, someone is going to get seriously injured or killed."

"I agree." Nodding, Henry stood and looked at Sabrina. "Now let's take a walk around the property like Sabrina suggested." He swung his gaze to Duncan.

"If any of you would like to stay here, you can stay in this room or join the rest of my pack in the large living room."

Duncan nodded. "I think we'll go talk to the crowd in the living room."

Everybody rose and followed Henry out of the room. Callum was debating whether to walk around the property with the beautiful woman who didn't like him or join Duncan and Julianne in the living room with the rest of Henry's pack. Meeting a whole pack like that and announcing his disability to everyone wasn't something he would normally do if given a choice, but walking around with a woman who obviously disliked him wasn't an attractive option either.

But for some reason, he didn't like the thought of Vamika walking around the grounds after what she had experienced with Ambrosia earlier, and particularly not when they had no idea where the evil witch was. She could be hiding somewhere just waiting to strike again, and he wanted to be there if she did.

He followed the others out of the house, staying a few steps behind them as he normally did. As soon as they exited the house, the other people adjusted their position to walk four abreast with Leith and Sabrina in the middle, but Callum stayed a few steps behind them. It gave him the opportunity to watch out for them from behind at the same time as it kept him out of Vamika's line of sight.

The large property was beautiful and green, and most of it consisted of lawns and houses interspersed with clusters of trees. The western perimeter was lined with a dense forest that could hide anything, and they walked next to it to let Sabrina check if she could pick up the power of the other witch. Callum wasn't sure what she meant by that, but he imagined it was a bit like the way he could pick up if someone was a shifter if they were close enough, except for him it was mostly their scent that alerted him to them not being human.

His gaze kept drifting back to Vamika's shapely body as she moved with a fluidity and grace that was enticing. She was smaller than average for a Scottish woman, but then her ancestors obviously weren't Scottish. Based on her colors and features, he would guess she was of Indian decent, but he wasn't going to ask her to check if he was right. He had already induced her wrath without even trying, and asking her about her heritage might be taken as disapproval or even harassment, at least when coming from him. He didn't really care where people were from. What mattered was what people were like. But she didn't know that, and she might not even agree. She didn't like him, and the main difference between him and the others was his disability, so the obvious conclusion was that she didn't like him because he was different.

No matter how Vamika felt about him, though, he couldn't seem to keep his eyes off her. Her braid was swinging from side to side, drawing his gaze to her swaying hips as she walked. And staring at her ass was not good for his sanity or his jeans. They were getting tighter in the groin area by the second, and he was happy he had chosen to wear a loose T-shirt that covered the outline of his hard cock.

They were approaching the house after spending half an hour crisscrossing the property. Sabrina hadn't picked up anything to indicate that Ambrosia was close by, but there was, of course, still a chance the witch was hiding in the forest. Leith hadn't wanted to venture in there to look for her, since it left them more open to a surprise attack, and shifting to scent the area was always a risk during the day.

Callum brought up the rear when they walked into the house. The others walked into the office, and he was just a couple of yards away from the doorway when Vamika came back out of the office and grabbed his hand.

"Come with me." It wasn't a request as much as a command.

He was too stunned to object and let her lead him into a room on the opposite side of the hallway from the office. It was a small cozy living room with a fireplace.

He was barely inside the room before she closed the door behind them. Then, she put her hands on his chest and pushed him against the wall. Her dark-brown eyes were almost black with fury as she stared up at him, and he realized just how short she was compared to him. The top of her head didn't even reach the height of his shoulders.

She pushed her index finger into the middle of his chest. "Don't think I will let you claim me no matter what we are to each other. I don't care." Her gaze didn't waver.

Callum felt himself frowning as he tried to understand what she meant. He'd had no intention of claiming her, so what was she talking about? Had she noticed how he had been staring at her ass while walking around the property? "I'm sorry, I—"

"No!" She tapped the tip of her index finger against

his breastbone. "I don't want your apologies or excuses. No wolf will own me. Ever! I don't care about true mates. It won't happen."

He shook his head slowly as he held her gaze. "Why are you telling me this?" He hadn't realized his admiration would be taken as a serious intention to claim her as his mate. Things were obviously quite different in this pack compared to what he was used to. Not that he was part of a pack, but it seemed strange.

"Enough with the arrogance!" She smacked his chest hard with her flat hand, and he winced at the impact. "Don't act like this is inevitable and that it will only be a matter of time. I don't care that we're true mates. I decided years ago that I'd never let anyone claim me, and I don't care that the universe decided to fuck with me like this. I'd rather die than be your mate."

Callum could only stare at her while her words whipped him with their intensity and harshness. *True mates, true mates, true mates.* His mind was reeling, and his body was pulsing with the knowledge that she was right. But this couldn't be happening. He had never even considered the possibility that he would meet his true mate, and to have her reject him outright at first sight without even trying to get to know him was threatening to drown him. He needed air. He needed to get away. He needed to throw up.

With a heart that was tearing open, he pushed her away before turning and ripping the door open. He stormed out of the house and started running. It was a stilted, awkward gait that he never showed people, but he didn't care at the moment. There was nothing to care about. His true mate didn't even want him; what was left for him then? Nothing.

He ran until his body was threatening to collapse if he didn't stop. Then, he bent over and threw up until there was nothing left in his stomach.

His mate was beautiful, the most beautiful woman in the world. With a backbone of steel and a fierceness fit for an alpha. But she didn't want him. He wasn't good enough for her. A young, medium power wolf with a handicap and no means to speak of. He wasn't exactly a catch in any sense of the word.

CHAPTER 20

Sabrina rose from the sofa when Leith did. There wasn't much more they could do for Henry and his pack. There was still a chance that Ambrosia was hiding somewhere in the area, but Sabrina hadn't been able to sense her. And without having met her in person, Sabrina's power wouldn't be enough to try to pinpoint the woman's location.

Perhaps Callum had some more information for them. He hadn't joined them in Henry's office when they returned to the house half an hour earlier, so he was probably hard at work on his laptop again. The man was nothing if not intelligent and resourceful. He had already been instrumental in saving Julianne from Ambrosia and Steven's clutches, and now that he had been able to identify the woman's phone, there was a real chance they would be able to catch up with her soon.

They followed Henry out of the house. His pack had returned to their houses and normal activities, and there were kids playing on the lawn like nothing special had happened just a few hours earlier. They had clear instructions not to go near the forest, but apart from that, they were back to normal.

"Where's Callum?" Duncan turned toward them with a frown. "I thought he'd be out here doing his surveillance things, but he's not in the car, and his laptop is still there."

Henry narrowed his eyes in thought. "Vamika's gone too. She said she'd be right back when she left the office, but she never returned, and she wasn't in the living room when I went to tell the wolves they could go back to their houses. She has a room upstairs. I'll go check if she's there and if she knows where Callum is."

Sabrina felt herself frowning. She didn't know Callum well, but he didn't seem like a person to just take off without saying something. And without his laptop. Something was wrong, she was sure of it.

"Duncan, would Callum approach Ambrosia on his own if he discovered where she was?" Sabrina looked at Duncan, who was studying the nearby forest like Callum might be hiding just out of sight.

Duncan turned to her and shook his head. "No, that's not like him. He'd tell us so we could go after her together. He's not the reckless type, if you overlook his hacking."

"That's what I thought." Sabrina nodded. The thought of losing Callum to Ambrosia was horrible. There was no telling what she would put him through. He would, of course, be expected to mate some woman of Ambrosia's choosing, but would that be possible without his consent? Sabrina didn't think so, but maybe Ambrosia had some ace up her sleeve that they didn't know about. And if Callum's fate at Ambrosia's hands wouldn't be bad enough, they would also lose their best means of finding her with Callum gone.

"Let us not assume the worst just yet." Leith's arm circled her waist, and he pulled her close. "I can see what you are thinking, but we have no indication that Ambrosia is behind Callum's disappearance. He might have simply gone for a walk."

"Well, he's not answering his phone, which is unlike him." Duncan pulled his phone from his ear. "I don't like this. He wouldn't just wander off without telling us."

Julianne cocked her head. "Could he have gone to talk to some of the families?"

Duncan shook his head. "I don't think so. He usually stays away from shifters he doesn't know. You saw how he was treated by the shifters we visited down south, and that wasn't bad compared to how he's usually treated. He was with us at the time, and I believe that kept some of the harsh comments and ridicule at bay. If he'd been alone, they might not have bothered to listen to what he had to say, let alone paid much attention to any of his advice. Having a weakness is barely tolerable in the shifter world, and a physical weakness is unacceptable. Callum has been treated badly his whole life. That he's turned into the decent young man he is, is nothing short of a miracle."

Henry came out of the house, trailed by Vamika. The woman's scowl was worse than usual, and Henry's expression was thunderous. "Tell the others what you told me, Vamika." His tone was hard and unforgiving, making it clear that his anger was directed at the woman following him.

Vamika stopped several yards away from them and crossed her arms over her chest. "Callum." She spat his name. "I just told him the truth. I will never be owned by anyone. If I ever choose to settle down, my mate will be human and not a shifter. I will never let a shifter touch me."

Sabrina felt her jaw drop in shock. She had been blaming Ambrosia for Callum's disappearance, but this had nothing to do with the evil witch. "He's your mate. Your true mate."

Julianne gasped and Duncan swore. Leith mumbled something under his breath.

"I don't care." Vamika's eyes were hard and black with her anger. "I will fight him if he ever tries to claim me, and if he manages to mate me, anyway, I will kill myself. I will never be his."

"Where is he?" Duncan stared at Vamika with a neutral expression on his face. "Where did he go?"

The woman shrugged. "I don't know. He ran off into the forest." There was a glimpse of concern in her eyes for half a second, but it was gone so quickly Sabrina wasn't sure it had really been there at all.

Duncan took a deep breath, like he was struggling for control. "Where did he enter the forest?"

Vamika pointed, and they all looked in that direction. There was, of course, nothing to see but forest, but at least they had the direction he had gone and the reason why he had left.

"If something has happened to him, I hope you will suffer." Duncan's words were harsh, but Sabrina understood why he uttered them. "He's my friend, and he's been through enough already without you destroying his life. I don't care why you don't want him. You're not worthy of someone like him, anyway. I just hope he lives through this to find a woman who will treat him right. He deserves that." Duncan swung his gaze to Henry. "I'll shift and go after him. If you have someone who can go with me that would be great."

Henry gave a sharp nod. "I'll go myself."

Sabrina was expecting Leith to say he would go as well, but he didn't. He wasn't a wolf, of course, but he was powerful. He'd most likely be able to help no matter what his shifter side was. Or perhaps not. She didn't have any idea what he was, and if he was something that couldn't run very well, he might not be much help in this situation.

Duncan and Henry started undressing, and Sabrina turned to look up at Leith. He was the only man she wanted to see naked, and just the thought made her pussy clench with need. It must have shown in her eyes because his eyes brightened into emerald immediately, and he pulled her into his arms.

His breath tickled her ear when he whispered too low for anyone else to hear. "Do not look at me like that. I am already struggling."

She couldn't help the small smile that crept across her face, and she buried her face against his chest to hide her expression from the others. This wasn't the time to smile.

Sabrina sighed. She had struggled with Leith being her mate at first and tried to stay away from him. The reasons she had for keeping him at an arm's length were sound, and maybe she understood better than most that there could be reasons to deny the mating bond that had nothing to do with your mate.

Rising on her toes, she put her cheek against Leith's and spoke in a low voice. "I'm going to try to talk to Vamika, if she'll listen to me."

Leith nodded against her cheek. "Okay."

Sabrina pulled out of his arms and turned toward the black-haired woman still scowling as she kept her eyes on the forest where Duncan and Henry had gone in search of Callum. Swinging her gaze to Julianne, Sabrina indicated she was going to talk to Vamika. Julianne nodded and moved over to stand beside Leith.

"Vamika?" Sabrina approached with what she hoped was a pleasant expression. She wasn't known for her sweet-talking skills, but then she didn't think Vamika would respond well to something like that, either. Sabrina preferred the direct approach, and she had a feeling Vamika did as well. "Can we talk?"

The woman narrowed her eyes at Sabrina. "I don't see the point."

"Maybe you don't, but I do." Sabrina didn't waver and walked right up to the woman without breaking their eye contact. "From what I understand, denying a true mate can have serious consequences, so I, for one, expect an explanation. And I believe you have one. This is not just a spur-of-the-moment decision for you. You have your reasons, and they're probably good ones. Mine were too."

Vamika looked surprised for a second before she reverted to her scowling. "I'm not going to change my mind."

"Perhaps not, but I think Callum deserves an

explanation if not the rest of us." Sabrina was aware that she hadn't wanted to tell Leith the reasons she didn't want to mate him, and they still weren't mated for some of those reasons.

Vamika looked toward the forest. "I have already told him I'll never let anyone own me. Not him, not anyone. What more is there to say?" Without giving Sabrina a chance to respond, the woman abruptly turned and headed toward the house, effectively ending their conversation.

CHAPTER 21

Callum didn't know how long he had been sitting propped against a tree, but it must have been a while. He just couldn't seem to get over the shock of being rejected so brutally, let alone the shock that he had a true mate. But why he was so surprised at being rejected was a mystery to him. It wasn't exactly the first time. Shifter women didn't want a man who wasn't fully functional, as one of them so harshly had told him, making him realize she thought he couldn't perform sexually because he had a limp. So, it hadn't taken him long to understand he'd never mate a female shifter.

Human women were completely different. He was tall and muscular, and relatively attractive. And he liked to pay compliments and make people feel good about themselves. Apparently, those were all great attributes in the eyes of human women, and despite his limp, he was soon a hit with the women in Fort William, getting more action than he had ever thought possible. It didn't take him long to understand that there was hope for him, even though no shifter female wanted him. Some shifters mated humans and were happy with that, and he would do the same.

He pulled in a deep breath and let it out slowly, trying to ease the tension in his body. Yes, he had happily dated several human women, but he wasn't sure that would be possible after meeting his true mate. Just the thought of touching another woman felt wrong to him, not in a moral sense but in the sense that it made him feel nauseous. If that persisted, he would have to stay away from dating altogether. Not that it was a big concern at the moment. What kept spinning through his mind was why. Why didn't Vamika like him? What had he done to make her despise him? Was it just his disability alone, or was there some other reason? So many questions were spinning through his mind, and he didn't know the answer to any of them.

Shaking his head, he tried to dislodge all the questions that were clogging his mind. And the self-doubt and negativity that he'd battled regularly for as long as he could remember. This wasn't the time to sink into that pit. It wasn't the first time someone rejected him, and it wouldn't be the last. It didn't matter that it was his true mate this time. He wasn't going to break. If she didn't want him, her loss. He was going to keep going like he always did.

Getting to his feet, he looked around. He was in the middle of the forest, and he had no idea where he was, but he knew he had been running in a westerly direction, so if he headed toward the east, he might end up where he started. Or at least he would hit the sea at some point, and he could take it from there. It was too bad he couldn't shift and follow his own scent back, but it was daylight, and he didn't want to accidentally be seen by someone.

He'd walked no more than ten minutes when two wolves bounded toward him. One of them was Duncan, but he didn't know the other one.

A second later Duncan was standing in front of him with a relieved expression on his face. "There you are. I was getting worried that we weren't going to find you."

"Well, here I am." Callum didn't have it in him to smile at the moment. The best he could give his friend was a blank expression. "I'm sorry for running off without saying anything."

Duncan narrowed his eyes as he studied Callum's face, probably to determine his state of mind. But Callum didn't have any intention of discussing what had happened, not even with Duncan, who was one of the most decent and supportive shifters he had ever met.

"Let's go, Duncan. I'm sure Julianne is anxiously awaiting your return." Callum stepped around his friend and started walking.

"Shift, Callum. Henry knows how to get back with a minimal chance of being seen."

Callum stopped and turned to face Duncan. "I haven't brought any extra clothes."

Duncan shook his head as amusement filled his eyes. "I guess you will have to sleep in the back of the car like a dog then." He frowned like he regretted making a joke. "I'm sorry. I'm sure someone can lend you a change of clothes when we get back."

"Okay." Callum nodded. "And no need to apologize, Duncan. I'm not made of glass." It was evident that Duncan knew what had happened with Vamika for him to act like this, but Callum didn't want to be treated any differently than he had been before. He just wanted everything to be normal, or as close to normal as possible.

He removed his phone from the breast pocket of his shirt before quickly undressing. After changing into his wolf, he picked up his phone with his teeth and followed Henry and Duncan at a fast trot through the trees. His phone had a solid cover and was waterproof so carrying it around in his mouth shouldn't harm it.

It didn't take them as long as he'd thought it would to get back, and when they emerged from the trees, Leith, Sabrina, and Julianne were outside waiting for them. Vamika was nowhere to be seen, but then he hadn't expected anything else.

Henry and Duncan changed back into their human forms and got dressed in their clothes, which were lying scattered on the grass. It made Callum realize how worried they had been about him to discard their clothes in a hurry like that.

Sitting down, Callum put down his phone before letting his tongue loll out of his mouth while he panted. It was a warm day, a bit too warm to be running around with a fur coat.

"I'll get you some clothes, Callum." Henry gave him a nod before heading into the house.

Duncan embraced his mate like they hadn't seen each other for days, and pain stabbed through Callum's heart at the sight. He would never have that with his true mate.

A couple of minutes went by before Henry came back out of the house, carrying a pile of clothes. But he wasn't alone. Vamika followed the alpha out of the house with a furious expression on her face, no doubt because Henry had ordered her to follow him.

Henry walked right up to Callum where he was still sitting on the lawn in his wolf form. "Here. There should be something in here that will fit you." Then, he turned to Duncan and Leith with their mates. "Let's go inside to allow these two some time to talk."

Callum stared after them as everyone but Vamika disappeared into the house. He didn't want to talk to the woman again and listen to her repeat her rejection, but apparently he wasn't left a choice in the matter.

She was standing about five yards away from him with her arms crossed over her chest, and she made no move to approach him.

A sudden thought struck him. He had felt her presence the second she had entered the office behind him, and it hadn't taken more than a few glances at her shapely ass for his cock to stand at attention. If she was affected by him the way he was affected by her, perhaps it was time to show her whom she had rejected.

Still in his wolf form he rose and stretched. Callum wasn't the size of a typical alpha, but he wasn't much smaller. In fact he was relatively large to be a medium power wolf.

Without warning he changed into his human form and walked slowly toward her. He let his gaze linger on her face as she got her first look at his body, and he wasn't disappointed. Her eyes widened as she stared at him, her gaze dipping to caress the length of his body.

He was already sporting a semi just from having her eyes on him, and when her gaze zeroed in on his groin, his cock quickly swelled until it was hard and throbbing.

He walked until there was no more than a yard between them before he stopped. Henry had wanted them to talk, but Callum didn't know what to say. Vamika had already told him she didn't want him, and trying to persuade her otherwise seemed pointless and maybe even counterproductive. It might be better to just leave her with the image of him on her retinas.

Without saying anything, he turned around and walked back to the clothes Henry had left for him. He found a pair of jeans that seemed to be his size and turned around. Vamika snapped her eyes up to his, having obviously stared at his ass. It boosted his confidence, and he slowly put on the jeans one leg at a time. His cock was still jutting from between his legs, and he made a show of how difficult it was to close the jeans over his hard length. It wasn't really a show, though. It was a tight fit, and when he winced at the discomfort, it was real.

Vamika was still staring at him, but instead of pure fury in her eyes, there was a mix of desire and fury. The combination was tantalizing, and before he realized what he was doing, Callum was walking back toward her. He didn't stop until he was directly in front of her, and her head was tipped back to hold his gaze.

"I don't care why you don't want me, Vamika. I want you anyway." Callum was a bit surprised at his own confident voice and the fact that he was speaking at all. He hadn't intended to say anything, but there he was telling her the truth. "You're the most beautiful woman I have ever seen, but even without your looks, I would've wanted you for your strength and fierceness. Too bad you don't want me. We could've been good together."

Without waiting for a response, that would no doubt have been in the form of a rejection, he took a step to the side before heading into the house.

∞∞∞

They were on their way back to Inverness. They were no closer to finding Ambrosia than they had been earlier that morning, and they had not been able to find out why she had visited Henry's pack again.

Leith sighed. He wanted this to be over. His body was in a constant state of arousal, and it was starting to get uncomfortable. All he wanted was to turn around and drive until he was sure they were far away from anyone. Once there he would beg Sabrina to mate him. He didn't think her magic would hurt him, not even with a higher dose than he had already received. And if it did, he would heal. Not mating soon would hurt more than whatever she could do to him with her magic. He was sure of that.

His phone rang. It was Callum, and Leith touched the phone symbol that appeared on the screen in the car to accept the call.

"Hi, Callum."

"Leith. Ambrosia just turned on her phone. She's at McFarquhar's Bed. Do you know where that is?"

Leith nodded, even though Callum couldn't see him. "Yes. We will head in that direction. Where are you?"

"No more than five minutes behind you. We stopped for gas. Trevor, Jennie, Michael, and Steph are on their way as well. I just talked to Trevor. They had just arrived in Inverness, but they were going to get back into their cars to meet us there." Callum's voice was a little harder than before, but then he had been through a lot in the last few hours. That the guy was functioning at all was incredible.

"Good. We will see you all there." Leith ended the call before glancing at Sabrina. "I guess this is it. Unless Ambrosia disappears again before we can get to her."

Sabrina nodded. "I'm ready for this to be over with, but we never got around to making a plan for how to approach her. I guess we'll just have to play it by ear. We don't know what she'll do when she sees us, anyway. She might run or she might fight. So far she has run whenever she's hit a snag, so that's the most likely scenario. But we can't count on it."

"You are right." Leith felt himself frowning. "The fact that she disappears whenever her plans do not pan out the way she has foreseen has me doubting her power. But it is most likely just caution and the fact that she is operating alone that has her running."

"Most likely, yes." Sabrina turned to him. "Which means we should try to prevent her from escaping this time. We will never be able to deal with her if she always disappears whenever we get close."

Leith met her gaze for a second. "Ambrosia will find it hard to run if she is down by the water at McFarquhar's Bed. It is a steep and craggy shoreline, and we will be accessing the area via the only path down. There are not a lot of places to go once you are down there. If that is where she is, she is not expecting anyone to come after her."

They drove as close as they could in the sports car and parked in the lane next to a few houses. It was only a few minutes' walk from there through the fields to the shore and McFarquhar's Bed.

"We should wait for the others before approaching Ambrosia." Leith turned to face Sabrina.

Frowning, Sabrina glanced at him for a second before looking toward the shoreline. "Let's walk closer. We don't have to approach her, but I'd like to check if I can see her and what she is doing here. It makes no sense to me why she would go somewhere like this. There has to be a reason."

"Okay." Leith nodded slowly and turned to look around. There were no people anywhere that he could see. "But we do not walk down there until the others arrive. There is no telling what she will do if she feels cornered."

"I agree." Sabrina opened the car door to get out, and Leith followed suit.

They walked toward the bushes marking the end of the field and the edge of the craggy slope down to the shore. Leith kept his gaze on the bushes and was prepared to protect Sabrina if he saw anyone. He had a fair idea of what Ambrosia looked like based on how people had described her, but he had never seen her. As far as he was concerned, it was better to be safe than sorry.

They reached the bushes, and Leith showed Sabrina where to go to be able to look down toward the shore. There were two people down there, a woman and a man, and from where they were standing, the scene that played out looked brutal.

The woman's hands were splayed on either side of the man's head, and from the obvious tension in his body, he looked to be in severe pain and unable to do anything to stop her.

"No," Sabrina whispered next to him right before she took off running toward the path that led down to the pair on the shore.

"Fuck!" Leith stormed after his mate and reached her before she could start the descent. Just the thought that his mate could get hurt filled him with dread. He gripped her upper arm and turned her to face him. "Sabrina, we have to wait for the others. I won't let—"

She shook her head firmly. "No, we don't have time for that. She'll kill him. I can't let her do that."

"Sabrina!" He hissed her name. "You are not allowed—"

Her eyes lit up with fury. "Don't even think about telling me that I'm not allowed to intervene. It's my choice, not yours."

She ripped her arm out of his grip and ran down the path, and he gritted his teeth in frustration as he hurried after her to make sure he was right there if she slipped.

It didn't take them long to get down to the shore, and the sight that met them was nothing less than horrible. The woman, who was clearly Ambrosia, stood over the crumpled body of the man she had been torturing. His head was turned to the side, so Leith couldn't see his face, but the side of his head was blackened like he had been in a fire, and the air was permeated with the stench of burnt flesh. It brought back memories that he immediately pushed to the back of his mind to be able to focus on Sabrina's safety.

Ambrosia turned toward them, and Sabrina stopped about fifteen feet away from the evil witch.

"Who is that?" Sabrina indicated the man on the ground while staring at the other woman.

A disturbing smile spread across Ambrosia's face, and she chuckled. It was a chilling sound that made Leith take a step closer to Sabrina. The urge to pull his mate behind his back to protect her was so strong he had to fist his hands at his side to prevent himself from acting on the need.

"He doesn't deserve a name." Ambrosia snarled the words as she stood there glaring at them.

Sabrina nodded slowly. "He killed your daughter."

Ambrosia's eyes narrowed in suspicion, and she took a step backward away from them, like she was preparing to flee.

"We talked to the pack this man used to belong to." Sabrina's voice was neutral, like this didn't affect her at all, and she was only recounting facts. "You gave your name to one of the pack members when you came looking for your daughter. He mated her against her will. She died. Now he's dead. Justice has been served."

Ambrosia shook her head slowly when Sabrina stopped talking. "No. This is not justice. This is only one small step toward justice. It took me a while to find him." She kicked the man's leg for emphasis. "Now I can concentrate on the work ahead."

"Ambrosia." Sabrina's gaze never wavered from the woman. "This is the man who took your daughter. He has clearly been dealt with. I wish that was enough to bring your daughter back, but unfortunately, it isn't. Nothing can bring her back, and hurting people will not change that fact. You know that."

The evil witch chuckled again. "Do I?" Her expression changed into one of disgust. "Beasts should not be allowed to live. They prey on whoever they want and use the excuse that you're their mate, and when you finally think your daughter is safe and will not suffer the same fate, they come for her as well. Nobody is safe until all beasts are eradicated, and that includes you."

Ambrosia's gaze swung to Leith, and her eyes changed into a cold pale-green color. He felt a push against his mind like something was trying to break through and take control, but before he could react, Sabrina stepped in front of him and the push disappeared.

Sabrina's hands were stretched out in front of her with her palms facing Ambrosia like a shield, and he could feel her power caress his skin. "You don't get to hurt him. He's mine."

Leith started when the evil witch burst out laughing. "Really? Are you sure it's not the other way around? You're so naïve. They like to make you believe they're yours, but it's a ruse, and it will soon become apparent that you're nothing but property to them, and by then it's too late."

Leith wanted to step to the side and push Sabrina behind him, but he couldn't. His feet were locked in place like he'd been nailed to the ground, and he had no idea which of the two women was responsible for that. It might be Ambrosia to stop him from charging her, or it could be Sabrina in order to protect him.

Leith opened his mouth to speak, but Sabrina spoke before he could. "I'm sorry your mate treated you badly, Ambrosia, but that doesn't mean every shifter is an asshole."

"You're a gullible fool." Ambrosia's eyes met his over Sabrina's head a second before power slammed into him, knocking him off his feet. It didn't hurt since he had expected something like that to happen and was using his own power like a shield around his body, but he still landed on his back as a result of the impact.

Sabrina gasped and whipped around. Her eyes met his, and he shook his head to tell her that he wasn't hurt.

"I'm fine. Don't worry—" His words were cut off by the suffocating power that surrounded him, but the magic wasn't directed at him.

The concern he might be hurt had snagged Sabrina's attention for too long, and she wasn't prepared when Ambrosia attacked. Sabrina's eyes widened in shock when her body was picked up, and before he could reach her, she was flung several yards away to land among the rocks in the water.

He heard himself shouting in disbelief and horror as he started running. An echoing shout came from somewhere up the slope from the beach, but he didn't have time to think about that.

Leith was by Sabrina's side in less than two seconds, and the sight that met him made his heart stutter. He had seen friends killed, cut almost in half by a sword, but that was nothing compared to this. The deep gash stretched from her forehead to her ear, blood pouring down her cheek. But it wasn't the sight of the gash or the blood that broke him; it was her staring, lifeless blue eyes.

There was nothing he could do. The headwound was too severe and help was too far away. Sabrina was already gone, and even Steph wouldn't have been able to heal her if she had been there.

There were voices behind him, and the sound of several people running toward him. But he didn't want them there. He didn't want their attention, their concern, or their grief. Sabrina was his. His mate, his love, his life. But she was gone, and he would soon be gone as well.

Leith lifted her limp body in his arms and waded into the sea until the water closed over his head. His clothes fell away in ripped pieces when he changed into his other form and started swimming with his mate clutched to his chest. He had no intention of ever surfacing again. All his hopes and dreams were gone, destroyed in one second. He had failed his mate, failed to protect her. And he couldn't live without her.

There were plenty of undisturbed places beneath the waves, and he would pick a remote place where they would never be found. Cradling his mate against his large body, he would lie down until he faded away, and together they would sink into the clay and sand on the ocean floor and be gone forever.

CHAPTER 22

Water. It was the first clear thought that penetrated the darkness that wanted to swallow her mind. She was in the water, and it felt good. Like coming home after being gone for a long time. It was strange. She had always loved the water, particularly when there were no people around and she could swim naked. Feeling the water caress every part of her body was soothing, and it always made her smile, no matter what she was struggling with at the time.

Sabrina pulled in a deep breath, except it wasn't air she was breathing. It was water. She probably would have panicked and started thrashing to get away from whatever was keeping her in the water if she'd had control over her body. But her body was limp, and she couldn't move a muscle, and that was another reason to panic. Screaming in her mind, she tried to force her body to obey her command to move, but nothing happened. The darkness at the edges of her mind that she had been trying to push back chose that moment to charge, and she sank back into blackness.

∞∞∞∞

Callum felt numb as he drove back toward Inverness. Duncan was sitting in the back trying to console his shattered mate. Sabrina had been her best friend, even though as far as Callum could tell, the two women were quite different.

Callum tried to focus on driving and let his mind take a break from everything that had happened that day. He didn't even know how to process everything yet. He'd found and lost his true mate at the same time. That itself was so overwhelming he had pushed it to the back of his mind to deal with later. It was the only way he could stay on his feet and do what was necessary.

Ambrosia turning on her phone had seemed like a lucky break, and he'd actually thought they would be able to get her. But as soon as he saw Leith's empty car near McFarquhar's Bed, he had gotten a bad feeling. Sabrina was a witch, and Leith was extremely powerful, but even so they should have waited for backup before confronting the evil witch.

Unfortunately, his fears weren't unfounded, as had become abundantly clear when they descended the slope and saw Sabrina's body fly through the air and land amongst the rocks like a broken doll. Callum didn't know whether it was Ambrosia's magic or the impact with the rocks that killed her, but even from a distance, there was no mistaking her lifeless stare. Sabrina was gone, and Leith's horrible howling noises only proved that fact.

Julianne's screams had combined with Leith's wailing as she ran toward her dead friend, and the terrible sound had made the small hairs on the back of Callum's neck stand up. Duncan was right next to his mate, his focus clearly divided between his distraught mate and the threat from Ambrosia.

The evil witch had slowly backed away, and Callum had considered going up against her. But his reasoning kicked in in time, and he realized that he was no match for her if she could win against Sabrina and Leith. He might even provoke her into attacking the others if he tried to take her on by himself, and they had enough on their plates at the moment as it was.

Leith had lifted his dead mate and carried her into the water without a word or a glance in their direction. The last they saw of him was the smooth gleaming back of an enormous sea creature curving out of the water before disappearing beneath the waves. Callum had never been told what Leith was, and he hadn't wanted to ask, figuring it was up to the man himself whether he wanted people to know. And in time Leith might have told him, but Callum had only met the man once before arriving at his house with Duncan and Julianne a few days ago.

After Leith and Sabrina were gone, they had stayed at the beach for more than an hour until Duncan had finally been able to persuade his mate to leave. Even if Leith survived the loss of his mate and chose to come back, there was no reason for him to wade ashore on that beach. Callum couldn't imagine Leith ever wanting to see the place again and be reminded of what happened there.

But the likelihood of Leith ever returning was

miniscule. At least that was Callum's opinion. The man would never recover. He would die soon, and neither Leith nor Sabrina would ever be found.

Trevor, Jennie, Michael, and Steph had arrived sometime after Leith had taken his mate and left, and they were, of course, just as shocked and horrified by what had happened as the rest of them. Their expressions said it all, even after their silence took over for their words of shock and sympathy.

None of them had expected this outcome. That Ambrosia would try to go after Jennie and Julianne, who were human, was something they had anticipated, and the women had agreed to stay in the background, but Sabrina was a powerful witch. Nobody had expected Ambrosia to be able to kill her so easily.

Shaking his head to clear it, Callum refocused on the road. Whether he should be driving at all with his mind everywhere but on the road was debatable, but then none of the others were in much better shape to drive. He could have asked Michael, but he doubted the man would be more focused at the moment with his mate in shock and feeling guilty for not putting enough emphasis on how powerful and dangerous Ambrosia really was.

They drove onto the Kessock bridge, and Callum breathed a sigh of relief. It wouldn't be long until they were at the hotel, and he could hide away in his hotel room for a while. He hadn't realized how he longed to be alone with his grief and shock until that moment, and suddenly the need to be far away from people was so strong it almost took his breath away.

The only thing he wanted more was to return to Vamika but he wasn't going to give in to that desire.

His true mate didn't want him, and he was going to respect her wish while silently hoping her body's need to mate would overpower her determination to stay away from him. He would probably know within about a week whether that was a possibility or not. Until then he would try to ignore his need for her and his own despair and shock that she refused him so brutally.

∞∞∞

Sabrina's eyes fluttered open, and she blinked a few times to clear them. Her cheek and the front of her body was pressed against warm silky scales, almost like snakeskin. Muscles were moving beneath the creature's skin while it moved in an undulating fashion, its body gliding through the water like a sine wave.

For some reason she could see just fine, even though there was no light shining through the water from above. And she didn't feel the need to breath. All those things should scare her, but she wasn't afraid. It felt natural and comfortable being in the water, and she felt safe being close to the creature.

Sabrina was pinned firmly against the warm body by what she assumed was a flipper, but one of her hands was free to move within the creature's embrace. Letting her palm glide over the smooth dark scales, she marveled at the velvety texture. It almost felt like the scales were covered by a thin layer of fur, as soft as that of a baby rabbit.

The creature made an abrupt move that broke the rhythmic sway of its body, and a huge slitted yellow eye was suddenly staring at her from three feet away.

She felt her jaw drop at the sheer size of the eye and the head filling almost her entire field of vision. It looked like some sort of dinosaur but kinder, if that made any sense.

Its mouth opened, and she stared at two rows of huge teeth that became visible. It might look like the creature was going to eat her, but she didn't think it would. There was something about the way its mouth curved up at the corners that made her think it was smiling at her like it was happy to see her. But that made no sense. Animals didn't smile. Not like humans, anyway.

A long pointy tongue suddenly thrust toward her and licked every part of her that wasn't covered by the flipper, shocking her more than the sight of the creature's huge eye. *What the hell?* Sabrina wanted to scream at it to behave, but what was the point of screaming at a dinosaur? She wasn't just going to meekly accept it, though. That was out of the question.

She pushed away from its body with her hand at the same time as she bucked her body. The creature's entire form shook like it had just been electrocuted, and she was suddenly free from its embrace. Kicking, she sped away from it at a much higher speed than she had anticipated, and she automatically looked down at her feet.

Sabrina had already been shocked several times since waking up, but nothing could have prepared her for the sight of her own body. Where her legs and feet were supposed to be, there was a long sleek fishtail. It was covered in iridescent scales and looked like something belonging to a quick and powerful fish.

Darkness crept into her vision, threatening to take

her consciousness, and she suddenly felt dizzy and nauseous. Something came around her back and scooped her up, and she was pressed against the same warm body as before. It felt so good to be comforted through the shock of what she discovered that she sagged against the creature's scaly soft skin and closed her eyes.

She shivered when her mind suddenly released thoughts and memories that pushed her experiences in the last few minutes out of the way. Sabrina had known whom she was the minute she opened her eyes, but the events from the last few days had not surfaced until this moment.

"Leith." She mumbled his name through the water in her mouth and fear shot through her, making her body tense. What had happened to him? He had seemed fine when she turned to him after he had been hit by Ambrosia's magic. But then the evil witch had picked her up and flung her through the air like she weighed nothing, and Sabrina couldn't remember anything after that.

She had to go back. Immediately. Leith could be injured, and she had to take care of him. Who knew what had happened after Ambrosia threw her into the air, but it was logical to conclude that the woman had attacked Leith as soon as Sabrina was out of the way. The bitch had said she wanted to eradicate all beasts, including Leith.

Sabrina bucked her body against the large flipper holding her, but this time the creature didn't let her go. It just tightened its hold on her and swam on. Swearing, she flattened her hands against its skin and let her magic flow into it. The creature shuddered and shook with the impact of her magic, but it soon recovered and kept swimming.

Light penetrated through the water, and she realized they were heading for the surface. Which was a relief. Although she wasn't sure what was going to happen to her when they broke the surface. She was a mermaid now, or at least something similar. Did that mean she could only live in the water from now on, or would she be able to breathe air as well? And what about her tail? It would be useless on land.

She raised a hand to her throat and used her fingers to glide over her skin until she felt the slits on the side of her neck. Gills. It shouldn't have come as a surprise, but she was still stunned to discover that she was more fish than human. Or maybe that wasn't correct. She was somewhere in between or perhaps both.

They broke the surface, and without thinking Sabrina spit out the water in her mouth and took a deep breath. Something moved in her throat, and her lungs filled with air like she hadn't just been using her gills to extract oxygen from the water.

They were close to the shore beneath some tall, rugged cliffs she didn't recognize. Not knowing how long she had been unconscious, it was impossible to say where they were, but she hoped they were still in Scotland. The sun was up, but it was quickly sinking toward the horizon. Darkness would cover this area soon, and she had a lot to do before that happened, one of them being finding a way to scale the cliffs above.

She was just about to try to get out of the creature's embrace again when the flipper fell away from her back, and strong arms enveloped her and pulled her against a familiar hard chest. It was so unexpected that she couldn't breathe for a second, but then a sob tore its way out of her chest, and she flung her arms around Leith's neck.

"Sabrina." His voice broke on the last syllable of her name, and he tightened his arms around her until he was almost crushing her. His face was buried in the crook of her neck, and his breathing was choppy like he was fighting not to cry.

"Leith." Sabrina felt her face split into a smile while tears coursed down her cheeks. "You're safe and you're a...monster." It sounded bad, but she didn't know what else to call him. No wonder he had wanted to postpone telling her what he was. He was no ordinary shifter. Leith had already alluded to the fact that he was different, but Sabrina hadn't realized the extent of *different* he was talking about. A wolf seemed somewhat mundane now, since she had met several wolf shifters in the last week, but Leith's animal was anything but ordinary.

"My angel. My sweet, extraordinary angel." He lifted his head from her shoulder, and their eyes met. Tears ran down his cheeks, and Sabrina felt her chest tighten with concern.

"Leith, what's wrong? You're crying." Her throat clogged with emotion, and her eyes leaked more tears in response to his. But they were no longer tears of joy and relief.

"Tears of joy, my angel. I lost you. You died, and I was bringing you to your final resting place. And mine as well. I could never go on without you." A smile curved his lips, and his eyes filled with a love so strong she could practically feel it beating against her chest.

"But then you woke, and you changed into the most beautiful creature I have ever seen. A mermaid. In all my years, I have never seen one of your kind. No wonder Aidan said you are unique."

"What do you mean I died?" Sabrina stared at him. The fact that she didn't remember anything after Ambrosia sent her sailing through the air meant that she had been knocked out. But she clearly hadn't died, so why did Leith think she had?

"Ambrosia hit you with her magic and threw your body several yards away. You hit your head hard against a rock when you landed, and even though I reached you within a couple of seconds, you were already dead."

Shaking her head, she frowned up at him. "I'm not dead."

He gave her a small smile. "And thank heavens for that. But you were. Perhaps immersing you in water was the right thing to do, and that was what revived you and changed you into your other form. A more resilient form. Mermaids live for centuries and do not die easily, just like aquatic beasts like me."

Taking a deep breath, she considered his words. It made no sense that she had been dead, and then suddenly she was alive again, but she didn't feel like getting into that discussion at the moment.

A sudden realization made her smile, and she couldn't believe how stupid she had been. Huge sea creature living by Loch Ness. She had, of course, just discovered that he was a huge aquatic beast, but she had known for several days that he was a special kind of shifter. She should have seen the connection. But she hadn't, until this moment. "You're Nessie, the

Loch Ness monster. Fuck, I'm stupid. I can't believe I didn't realize that earlier."

He tipped his head back and laughed, and her whole body tightened in response to the downright sexual sound. Before she could think better of it, she wrapped her legs around his waist and pulled his head down for a kiss.

CHAPTER 23

Leith tasted her lips and let his own slide against hers in a gentle caress. But his body was heating up fast, and his need for her wouldn't be denied after everything that had happened that day. She was his, and he wanted to make sure she stayed that way for all eternity.

Pulling his head back, he stared into her eyes. "I want to claim you. To make you mine. And this is as good a place as any to do so. It's remote, and the likelihood of there being people close by is very low. Will you allow me to make you mine, my angel?"

Sabrina's fingers moved into his hair, massaging his scalp. "On one condition. That you allow me to claim you as well. I don't know if it works the same for a mermaid, but I'll do whatever comes natural to me. Don't be surprised if I bite you too." Her brows pulled together in thought. "Or is that how you will claim me? By biting me, I mean."

His grin felt like it was splitting his face in two it

was so wide, and he wanted to yell with joy. But instead he nodded. "I will bite you when you start coming. As far as I know my bite will make you come harder. I will be gentle, but I have to break the skin and taste your blood."

She nodded and pulled his head down to her. Just before their lips met, she murmured. "Then let's get started. I want you."

Leith crushed his lips to hers and thrust his tongue into her mouth. But she didn't let him dominate her mouth for long. Her tongue dueled with his and stroked against it in a way that sent more blood south to his already hard cock. He rocked his hips against her, his hard length sliding against her hot, wet pussy. His body was pushing him to thrust into her tight sheath and claim her immediately, but he resisted. This wasn't just about claiming her as his; it was about love and starting a life together that would last for centuries. He would take his time to show her how much he loved her, even if his balls turned blue in the process.

She moaned into his mouth, before breaking their kiss and staring up at him. "I need you." Rocking her hips against him, she moaned again. "My whole body is screaming at me to claim you."

Leith grinned. "Well I guess that answers your question of whether mermaids mate." He stared into the glowing silvery blue of her eyes, his new favorite color.

He took her to the base of the cliffs and found a small patch of fine sand nestled between the rocks by the water's edge. It would be their mating bed, and a place he would take her back to every anniversary of their existence. It was a place not easily accessible to humans. The only way down the cliffs was by abseiling, unless you were a world-class rock climber, and boats couldn't get near the shore without the risk of getting slammed against the jagged rocks. Even swimming would be risky with the rocks penetrating the water. It was the perfect place for two sea creatures who wanted to spend some time alone together.

He kneeled in the soft sand before laying the beautiful woman in his arms down on the ground before him. She was, if possible, even more beautiful than before, like unlocking her other form had somehow enhanced her human appearance as well. But her appearance was just one of the aspects he loved about her.

When they met she had been reserved and made sure to keep him at a distance, but the reason wasn't because she considered herself better than him or didn't care about his feelings. In fact it was the opposite. Sabrina sacrificed her own wants and desires to make sure everyone else was safe. She wanted to make sure she never ended up in a situation where she could hurt someone. It was the reason for her tight control of her feelings and her, at times, stand-offish behavior.

"You're staring at me." There was a small smile on her lips, but her expression was one of uncertainty. "Is there something wrong? Do I have something on my face?" She chuckled like she wanted to cover the insecurity of her questions, but the sound was flat and joyless.

Leith smiled down at her. "I was just thinking about all the reasons I love you. So much has happened in just a few days, and not all of them good. But the result is perfect. I am the luckiest man alive to have found my other half. My true mate, who is more magnificent than I could ever have dreamed of. The most beautiful and selfless creature I have ever met, not to speak of her talents in bed." He winked at her, his grin widening. "Getting out of bed in the morning is going to be a real challenge with you around. I may have to tie you up and keep you there for days to have my fill, but I fear it would only feed my addiction and increase my need for you even more."

She laughed. "I love your words, but I think you should talk less and act more, my love." Her hand closed around his swollen member, and his whole body jerked in response to her touch.

His focus narrowed down to her body and his own. Need like he had never felt before slammed into him, and he pumped into her tight grip on his dick. Her other hand closed around his balls, massaging them gently, and it was all it took to bring him right to the edge.

"Stop!" He gripped both her wrists. "Or I will come, and I do not want to come until I claim you as mine."

Sabrina grinned up at him with amusement in her eyes. She knew exactly how close he was and was enjoying what she was doing to him. But thankfully, she listened to his plea and let go of him.

He wasn't going to let her off that easily, though. Without warning he buried his face between her legs and thrust his tongue into her tight channel. She yelped in surprise, and her body froze, but it only lasted for a second. Then, she lifted her pelvis and moaned as he moved his tongue around inside her, rubbing against her sensitive walls until he found that spot that made her hips jerk against his face.

He wrapped an arm around her hips to keep her in place before using his other hand to spread her folds and expose her clit. He rubbed her swollen pleasure button between his thumb and index finger, and her channel clamped down on his tongue. Her hips rocked against his face as she screamed her pleasure to the heavens, and a second later, he whimpered as magic shot into him. Her hands weren't even touching him, but her magic still entered his body and caused pleasure to spin through him like she had just taken all of him down her throat again. His whole body jerked with his orgasm as he sprayed his seed on the sand in powerful spurts. So much for not coming until he claimed her.

Before his breathing evened out, Sabrina pulled out of his hold on her and pushed him down onto his back. She straddled his hips, and he made a feeble attempt to explain that he might need a minute to recover. But she just shook her head and put her hand on his softening cock. "I want you inside me, and I don't think I can wait any longer. The orgasm you just gave me was amazing, but it did nothing to satisfy the deep ache inside me that will only be fulfilled with us mating."

Her power entered his body through his dick, but her magic was softer than he had experienced earlier. It was more than enough to get his blood flowing, though, and in just a few seconds, he was hard as steel and aching to be inside her.

***

Leith stared up at her with his beautiful emerald eyes shining with his desire. His cock was hard as steel under her palm, and Sabrina wanted to take him into her mouth. But she needed him inside her more. There would be plenty of time to pleasure him with her mouth later.

Her whole body was burning with bone-deep desire to feel him inside her. She'd never felt anything like it, and she had no will to deny her need. Her gums were itching to bite him, which was a strange feeling, and she needed him buried to the hilt in her weeping channel before she bit into his flesh.

"My angel." Leith's voice was rough with need, and it sounded more like a plea than an endearment. His need to claim her was right there in his eyes, and her channel clenched in response, telling her in no uncertain terms to get on with it.

"I need you too." She adjusted her position above him and gripped his cock. Moaning, she rubbed the head of his cock against her entrance before bringing it forward to slide over her sensitive clit. She was almost ready to blow by that small touch alone, but her channel ached with the need to be filled and tie Leith to her forever.

Strong hands gripped her hips, and before she realized what he intended she was on her back with his hard member thrusting into her until he was buried deep. "You are mine." The words were snarled at her. He pulled out before thrusting back inside, his long, thick cock filling her as perfectly as if her body had been used as a mold to make his. "I need you."

"Take me. Hard." Lifting her hips in encouragement, she stared into his glowing eyes.

"Good girl." He grinned at her, or at least she assumed that was what his grimace was supposed to be, but it looked too feral to really qualify as a smile. Pulling out of her, he gripped her legs and hooked her knees over his shoulders. "Ready?"

"Yes." The word was barely audible through her moan of anticipation.

Leith's hips shot forward to slam his hard length into her, and she felt her fingers and toes curl with the pleasure he created inside her.

"Again." She choked on the word, but he obviously understood what she wanted.

His hips started pumping with a furious pace, and all she could do was hold on as her lower belly tightened with a heat that promised to consume her. It felt so good, and she needed him so badly.

The orgasm took her by surprise, and she screamed Leith's name as pleasure radiated from her core and filled her body. Teeth sank into her shoulder, making her gasp with pain and bite into Leith's shoulder until hot blood filled her mouth.

White-hot pleasure tightened her whole body, and Leith screamed her name as his cock jumped and painted her insides with his hot cum. It seemed to go on forever with wave after wave of the most intense pleasure she had ever felt, being torn from her until darkness took her vision and she fell into blackness.

∞∞∞∞∞

Sabrina didn't know how long she had been out cold when she came to. But it must have been a while. It was dark and stars were twinkling in the night sky, clearly visible this far from people and artificial lights.

Leith's big body was lying on top of her, his heartbeat strong and even against her chest. But the weight of his body wasn't crushing her. Even without testing her strength, she knew she was stronger than before. She had no idea how powerful mermaids were compared to other shifters, but she would find out as she became more accustomed to her own strength and abilities.

Sabrina lifted her hand and buried her fingers in Leith's silky hair. His head was resting on her shoulder, and his even breaths were tickling her ear.

They were mated. A surge of happiness bubbled up inside her, and she laughed out loud with joy. He was hers. For years she had believed she would never marry or have a significant other in her life. It just wasn't possible for her. But here she was mated to the most fantastic man she had ever met, who happened to be a Scottish legend and a perfect match to her own sea creature.

"I think you broke me. I have never blacked out from sex before." Leith chuckled against her ear. "But then I've never mated a mermaid before."

Sabrina laughed. "I could say the same thing. Except replacing mermaid with the Loch Ness monster. No wonder I'm so worn out. I've been seduced by a monster."

Leith lifted his head from her shoulder and grinned down at her. "But it does not sound like that was a hardship." He lowered his head and gave her a lingering kiss before raising his head again to frown at her.

"What?" Her brows pulled together as she stared at

him.

"We should get back to the others. I am sure they are all shocked and distraught, particularly your friend Julianne."

Sabrina felt her eyes widen as she realized what he was saying. "They think I died. But how do they know? They weren't there yet. Did you wait for them to arrive before you took me away?"

He shook his head. "They arrived just as Ambrosia threw you into the air. I heard their screams, but I didn't pay them any attention. You were more important, and then my shock and grief took over. I left with you before they reached us, but I am sure they realized you were dead. I could hear it in their screams, even though I did not focus on their words at the time."

"Then we need to get back." Sabrina pushed at his heavy body to make him move, but he didn't budge. "Move!"

"Please listen to me first." He held her gaze. "We have no clothes, money, or phone. Swimming into Inverness and running through the streets naked is not an option. But we are less than ten miles from a panther clan. They will help us."

∞∞∞∞

Leith was still in shock and awe over everything that had happened in the last twenty-four hours. They were sitting in the backseat of a car going to Inverness. Or he was sitting, and Sabrina was sleeping with her head resting in his lap. Apparently, it was hard work dying, waking from the dead, changing into a mermaid, and mating a monster all within a few hours.

The panther clan had been happy to help them both with clothes and access to a phone. In return they had sat down with the panther alpha and recounted their latest experiences with Ambrosia. The alpha himself was mated, but there were several unmated panthers in his clan, and he wanted to make sure they were aware of the danger. There was no doubt that Ambrosia would continue to target shifters, and she was more powerful and brutal than they had expected.

But before they had sat down with the alpha, Sabrina had called Julianne. The woman had been shocked to put it mildly, crying and shouting with joy and disbelief until Duncan had snatched her phone and told them to hurry back to Inverness before Julianne and Duncan were thrown out of the hotel for disturbing all the other guests.

"Are you all right back there?" Ewan glanced at Leith in the mirror. The single panther had been kind enough to offer them a lift to Inverness. Ewan was going to go to Inverness, anyway, but he hadn't planned on leaving until later in the day. Since they were eager to go, though, he had offered to leave early, enabling them to get back to Inverness around midday.

"Yes. Thank you, Ewan." Leith nodded at the man in the mirror. "We appreciate your offer to leave early. My mate wants to make sure her friend is well. She was more than a little hysterical on the phone."

Ewan frowned. "I can imagine. It must've been a shock to see her friend die, and then to realize she wasn't dead after all. Two shocks so close together can render any person a bit hysterical, I think."

Leith nodded again. They hadn't told the panthers

the truth about what they were, only an abbreviated version fit for general consumption among shifters. "I believe you are right. But Julianne has her mate to take care of her. She will be fine."

They soon arrived in Inverness, and Leith shook Sabrina gently to wake her. "We will be arriving at the hotel in a couple of minutes, my angel. It is time to wake up and face Julianne."

Sabrina pulled in a deep breath before she opened her eyes and sat up. "Yes, I hope she's better now than she sounded on the phone." She sighed and turned to him. "I've never seen her so worked up. Not even when she realized that Steven had been tracking her. It was a good thing she could see my face, or I don't think she would've believed it was really me she was talking to."

Ewan stopped right outside the main entrance of their hotel, and they thanked him again as they got out of the car.

Leith grabbed Sabrina's hand and pulled her close. "I need a kiss before we face the others. Who knows when I will be able to have you all to myself again." He let his gaze roam her immaculate appearance. She had been sleeping only minutes before, but there was no evidence of that on her face. But he'd been told years ago that it was one of the typical traits of a mermaid. A flawless appearance at all times, not requiring much of an effort.

Laughing, Sabrina put her arms around his neck and stared up into his eyes. "I'll make sure it won't be too long, and I'm sure Duncan will help. He'll lure Julianne away before long with the promise of sex, and she won't be able to resist."

"Good." Leith bent his head and brushed his lips against hers. "Because it has been hours since we mated, and I want you all to myself again to have my wicked way with you."

A squeal from the hotel entrance alerted them to Julianne's arrival, and they barely had time to let go of each other before she flung her arms around them both and hugged them hard. Words poured from her mouth, but they were so garbled by her sobbing that Leith didn't understand what she was saying. It didn't matter, though. She was clearly happy to see them despite her crying.

Duncan appeared behind Julianne. With a grin a mile wide and amusement shining in his eyes, he put his hand on her shoulder. "You're getting snot all over them, sweet pea."

Julianne lifted her head from Sabrina's shoulder and stared down at the wet stains on her shirt. "Shit, I am." Then she lifted her head and met Sabrina's tear-filled gaze. "But you died on me. Don't ever do that again. I won't allow it."

Sabrina burst out laughing. "I'll do my best to prevent it, then."

"As will I." Leith smiled.

Julianne's eyes widened when she looked up at him. "You can smile."

Leith laughed.

"And you can laugh." Julianne's gaze snapped to Sabrina. "What did you do to him?"

Sabrina shrugged and grinned. "I mated him."

EPILOGUE

Sabrina let her eyes take in the beautiful man standing by the coffee machine. Tall and lean with corded muscles contouring his arms, and she knew the same was true for the rest of his body, which was currently hidden by his clothes. Long copper-colored hair was framing his gorgeous features, and his dark-green eyes were made for her to drown in. Her mate. And the most amazing man she had ever met. She was incredibly lucky.

But it wasn't just Sabrina who had been lucky in love. Julianne had been as well. The two friends were both mated and sated so to speak. There was no doubt that their vacation in Scotland had turned into the most life-altering time of their lives.

Sabrina couldn't help chuckling when Leith placed two steaming cups of coffee on the table, one for her and one for himself. The man was addicted to coffee, and she had a feeling one of the main reasons he was happy to be home was being reunited with his coffee machine.

"I get the feeling you are laughing at me, my angel." Lifting an eyebrow at her, he sat down next to her at the kitchen table. It was early morning, and nobody else was up yet.

"You're not mistaken." Sabrina grinned at him. "Your love of coffee is almost enough to make me jealous."

A small smile lifted the corner of his mouth. "Is that so? Do I have to show you again how much I want you?" His arm snaked around her waist, and he pulled her and her chair closer to him before he captured her lips in a slow kiss.

She leaned into him as their kiss deepened and her blood heated. They had spent a lot of time in bed since they got back from Inverness the day before, but it still wasn't enough. Just one look or touch was enough to make her body tighten with need. And now that he had proved he could absorb, and enjoy, all the power she sent out during her climax, there was nothing preventing them from staying in bed all day if that was what they felt like.

Her hand found the hard ridge in his pants and gave it a squeeze. Leith's body tensed, and he groaned as he broke their kiss and stared at her with glowing emerald eyes. "If you are trying to make me forget my coffee, you are succeeding. It should prove to you that you have no reason to be jealous of the beverage."

Laughing, she gave his cock another squeeze before pulling her hand away. "Just making sure, that's all, but I'll let you have your coffee now."

He narrowed his eyes at her like he was irritated, but he made no attempt to hide his amusement. "I do not think coffee will satisfy my craving at the moment. I would much prefer another taste on my lips."

Her channel clenched in response to his words, and she was just about to suggest they go back to bed when a sound in the hallway alerted her to someone coming.

Julianne and Duncan entered the kitchen hand in hand and smiling.

"Ah, there are the two lovebirds." Julianne's smile widened.

Sabrina burst out laughing. "That's funny coming from you. Like you guys haven't been sneaking off to your room every few hours."

Duncan tried for a haughty expression, but there was too much amusement in his eyes to pull it off. "I reserve the right to fuck my mate whenever she wants me to, thank you very much. And for your information, we still haven't fucked on the kitchen table, taking into consideration that you thought walking in on us doing that would be awkward."

Leith's eyes widened in surprise. "Yes, please refrain from doing that in my house. That's something better reserved for when you get home. Unless Trevor and Jennie object, of course."

As if on cue, Trevor and Jennie walked into the kitchen. "What is it we might object to?" Trevor lifted an eyebrow at Leith before swinging his gaze to Duncan.

They all laughed, leaving Trevor and Jennie to look from one to the other with a suspicious look on their faces.

Duncan took pity on them. "Leith wants us to fuck on the kitchen table when we get home."

"That is not—" But Leith's objection was cut off by Jennie's gasp.

"No! Forget it." Trevor narrowed his eyes at Duncan, obviously realizing who was behind the vulgar joke. "It's our table, so we're the only couple who gets to fuck on it."

"Trevor." Jennie gasped and smacked her mate's arm while the rest of the room erupted with laughter.

"Is it safe to come in, or are you all fucking on the table?" Callum's calm voice came from the doorway. "It looks like a sturdy table, but damn."

The laughter flared up again, and Sabrina felt like some of the heaviness in the air from the last few days shifted and took flight. And it felt good.

Ambrosia was still out there somewhere, planning to destroy shifters. She hadn't turned on her phone since they confronted her two days ago, which might mean she knew how they found her. But they weren't going to give up. They were going to find her and destroy her, and if anyone was supporting the evil witch, they were going to destroy those people too.

Michael and Steph walked into the room just as the laughter died down, and Jennie recounted the last few minutes' antics, which had made them all laugh and lightened the mood.

"Well, who wants coffee?" Leith stood and looked around at each person in the room. "I think I need some extra strong brew to wipe my mind of all the filthy stuff you people intend to do on top of perfectly innocent kitchen tables."

∞∞∞∞

Callum sat down on the bed in the room he had been given on the bottom level of Leith's house. It was a beautifully decorated room, just like the rest of the house, but he found it hard to be impressed by anything at the moment.

He wanted to leave and let the couples be. So many couples and all newly mated. They deserved to be happy, and he did his best to seem happy around them and pretend that he hadn't just had his heart crushed. But his patience was wearing thin.

Before meeting his true mate, he would have thought it strange to have your heart crushed by someone you'd just met. But that was before he realized the power and pull of a true mate. If she instead of rejecting him had thrown her arms around him and suggested they'd mate right there, he would have happily accepted. He wouldn't have needed any time to think about it after realizing that she was his true mate.

But Vamika had rejected him. He didn't know exactly why, apart from her excuse that she didn't want to be owned. But it wasn't a stretch to assume it had something to do with his disability. Few shifters accepted him unconditionally for whom he was; in fact, half of those who did were in Leith's house at the moment. There were a few more who tolerated his presence without openly complaining. But most shifters didn't even want to be in the same room with him, acting like his disability was somehow his fault and like there was a possibility it was contagious.

It would have been better if he had never met his mate at all. Then he would have been able to live a good life and perhaps mated a human woman who didn't care about his disability. Unfortunately, that wasn't an option anymore. The thought of any other woman than Vamika in his bed filled him with disgust, and there was no way he could even contemplate mating someone other than her. His life was forever altered, and he'd have to find a way to live with that.

Callum had heard the tales of people going crazy or even dying because their true mate rejected them or died, but he didn't really believe it. Someone could die from a broken heart. It happened to humans as well, occasionally. They simply gave up living and faded away. But that wasn't the same as dying as a result of the mating bond pulling you toward a person who didn't want you. Yes, his heart was broken at the moment, but he intended to live through it, and in time perhaps even conquer the bond and its effect on him. He was alive and had fought his whole life to stay that way, and he sure as hell wasn't going to give up just because some black-haired beauty decided he wasn't good enough.

∞∞∞∞

Vamika didn't know how long she had been sitting in her room, staring at the wall. Her mind and body were in utter turmoil, constantly pushing her to find Callum.

A shudder ran through her as the image of him walking toward her naked flashed in her mind again. Tall and muscular, with warm brown eyes turning golden as his cock hardened. His features were like those she imagined a Nordic god would have, with high cheekbones and a sharp jawline. And short blond hair in a messy hairstyle. The man was sex on a stick, stunningly perfect in every way, and his slight limp did nothing to retract from his perfection. That she'd been able to resist jumping him right there and then was a miracle. Because that was what she had wanted to do.

And it wasn't just his face and body that was perfect either. His calm demeanor and inner strength had called to her, trying to convince her that this man was different. That he would be a caring and decent mate who would treat her right.

She chuckled, but it came out bitter and angry. Like she would ever believe a male shifter wouldn't turn into a dominating and degrading asshole as soon as he was mated. From her experience that was mating in a nutshell. As soon as a woman had given in to the seemingly loving man wooing her, he turned into an asshole who wanted his woman shackled to his bed for his pleasure. Her desires and dreams didn't matter anymore. It was all about him and what he wanted.

And that wasn't going to be her life. Not even meeting her true mate, something that had shocked her to her core, could convince her otherwise. If she was going to mate anyone, it would be a human, even though the mere thought left her cold and mildly nauseous.

She rose from her chair and walked over to the window. It was a gray day with low, dense clouds and regular downpours, and it fit her mood perfectly. She needed to change and run until she was too exhausted to do anything other than fall into a deep sleep, but she had to wait until dark. It was always a risk running during the day, and Henry had been very clear that they were only allowed to do that if there was an emergency. And she concurred. Although, the risk of being seen was lower on a day like this when humans preferred to stay inside.

The image of Callum in all his naked glory flashed in her mind again, and she shivered when her channel clenched in response. Her body was begging her to go to him and let him sate her hunger, but that wasn't going to happen. She would just have to endure the frustration of being constantly turned on until it faded. Hopefully, that wouldn't take too long, because it was starting to get annoying. Particularly since getting herself off didn't seem to alleviate her need for more than a few minutes.

"Why did I have to meet you now?" She stared out of the window, no longer seeing the scenery outside. "When things are finally looking up, and fear isn't a constant companion anymore. I hate you, Callum. I hate you so much." But even as she said the words, she knew they weren't true. And that was what scared her the most.

---THE END---

BOOKS BY CAROLINE S. HILLIARD

Highland Shifters

A Wolf's Unlikely Mate, Book 1
Taken by the Cat, Book 2
Wolf Mate Surprise, Book 3
Seduced by the Monster, Book 4
Tempted by the Wolf, Book 5
Pursued by the Panther, Book 6
True to the Wolf, Book 7 – May 2023
Book 8 – TBA

Troll Guardians

Captured by the Troll, Book 1
Saving the Troll, Book 2
Book 3 – TBA

ABOUT THE AUTHOR

Thank you for reading my book. I hope the story gave you a nice little break from normality.

I have always loved reading and immersing myself in different worlds. Recently I have discovered that I also love writing. Stories have been playing in my head for as long as I can remember, and now I'm taking the time to develop some of these stories and write them down. Spending time in a world of my own creation has been a surprising enjoyment, and I hope to spend as much time as possible writing in the years to come.

I'm an independent author, meaning that I can write what I want and when I want. I primarily write for myself, but hopefully my stories can brighten someone else's day as well. The characters I develop tend to take on a life of their own and push the story in the direction they want, which means that the stories do not follow a set structure or specific literary style. However, I'm a huge fan of happily ever after, so that is a guarantee.

I'm married and the mother of two teenagers. Life is busy with a fulltime job in addition to family life. Writing is something I enjoy in my spare time.

You can find me here:
caroline.s.hilliard@gmail.com
www.carolineshilliard.com
www.facebook.com/Author.CarolineS.Hilliard/
www.amazon.com/author/carolineshilliard/
www.goodreads.com/author/show/22044909.Caroline_S_Hilliard

Printed in Great Britain
by Amazon